3 HE, ms, Hist
qual for vai ?? 24

26/. 12 o Lote Richardsairl
                27
      Lote accendum ?...
                62-3
9) Archie no speak /6
134 misc/records

D1333565

The Shoe

The Shoe

Gordon Legge

Polygon
EDINBURGH

© Gordon Legge 1989
Polygon
22 George Square, Edinburgh

Set in Linotron Sabon by
Polyprint, Edinburgh and
printed and bound in Great Britain by
Redwood Burn Limited, Trowbridge, Wiltshire

British Library Cataloguing in
Publication Data
Legge, Gordon
The Shoe.
I. Title
823'.914 [F]

ISBN 0 7486 6080 1

Dedicated to my Father and to the
memory of my Mother.

One

'Buy a couple of fags, mister?'

The enquiring youth wore Wrangler jeans and a Wrangler jacket. The jacket sadly failed to reach his wrists. His T-shirt read AC/DC. You could smell the shampoo and talc, see the shiny hair and smart trainers but he was still a Heavy Metal fan; he'd rather have been scruffy. He had acne. Bad acne.

'Don't bother. It's okay,' said Archie, declining the offer of 16p as he handed the youth two Benson and Hedges.

'Save your money and buy some cream,' scorned The Mental Kid.

'Thanks,' said the Heavy Metal fan, embarrassed by The Kid's remark. He lit the cigarettes using a disposable green lighter and returned to his two friends in the next carriage, handing one of the cigarettes to the smaller of the two, who in turn nodded and smiled appreciatively at Archie.

'Heavy Metal,' mused The Kid, 'it's okay if you don't have a brain, I suppose.'

Archie smiled at The Kid's smug disdain while wondering if it was worth getting upset at being called 'mister'. The previous Friday, a door-to-door salesman had asked if his wife was in. Archie had blushed and said 'No'. They never asked that. It was always 'Is your mother in, son?' And now a fat, ugly (Archie had decided to get upset) Heavy Metal fan called him 'mister'. Twenty-four next month. Older than Johnny Marr and Pat Nevin.

'Who was playing in Edinburgh tonight, anyway?' asked Mental, three months Archie's junior.

Archie shrugged a don't know don't care whilst wondering how old The Kid looked. Pretty rather than handsome, punky rather than cool; the triumph of content over style. The Kid wore a black Royal Navy raincoat, Levi's slit at the right knee, black Doc Marten shoes and a Celtic scarf, which until a couple of years ago he had worn with the regularity of a birthmark; now he only wore it for the Hun games and when it was cold. After every Celtic defeat he would begin the post-mortem with the words, 'What a nightmare. I was going *mental*!' The Kid's concession to ageing was an increased dependency on cliché. But he was still too lean and gorgeous to be addressed as an adult. The Kid leaned forward, resting his elbows on his knees while tapping his fingers in accompaniment to the noise of the train. Bored out of his skull, like.

'What time is it?' he asked.

'11.18.'

'Okay. So we get food and drink, go to the Apollo, watch the fights, more food and drink then home.' Mental related the forthcoming events as if he were a hesitant bank robber. Mental didn't like Glasgow and he didn't like staying up all night. Were he a bird, he would have chosen to be a budgie. 'If the Hun had brought his van we wouldn't have had all this hassle.' The Kid referred to the sleeping hulk across the hallway.

Big Davie looked married (within the year it was expected he would be) and he looked twenty-four (which he was): a 'mister'. Big Davie wore an old man's bunnet (10p from a jumble sale), a quilted blue jerkin, brand new Levi's and brand new Sambas. Solid rather than fat, a team man rather than an individual. The Daihatsu van remained at home so that Davie could have a drink on his night out. He couldn't be arsed driving to Glasgow, anyway.

'Work does that to you,' said Mental pointing a derisory

finger at the sleeper. 'Fat bastard!' shouted The Kid, hoping, but failing, to wake Davie.

Work was laying insulation for the council. Ten weeks into a six-month job, Davie hated it, but needed the money. He shared a private flat with his fiancée, Terasa.

Mental had never worked in his life. After school he attended college for three years, switching courses continually until one day he had the flu and never went back. The Protestant work ethic was anathema to him.

Archie left school at eighteen with three Highers: English, Modern Studies and a crash course History. His father was disappointed with Archie staying on at school. 'Get a trade, an apprenticeship. You'll always have it to fall back on.' Archie asked what the difference between a twenty-year-old tradesman and a fifty-year-old tradesman was. An argument ensued. Arguments never seemed to resolve anything, never a means to an end. Just an outburst of frustration. The father thought in terms of the home rather than holidays, relatives rather than friends, and work rather than play. Archie didn't know what he wanted, but when Morrissey sang about never having had a job because he was too shy, Archie understood, while his father would never know or admit to knowing.

For Archie, work had been a petrol pump attendant, a double-glazing salesman and a brickie's labourer. He had been unemployed for three years. The work provided fond memories and a few anecdotes but at the time it all seemed embarrassment and confrontation. He didn't know if he would ever work again; he supposed he would.

As the train neared Croy, the three Heavy Metal fans prepared to disembark. The small one who had smiled at Archie wore a beautifully battered leather jacket. He carried a poly-bag from which a rolled-up poster projected. Archie guessed that the bag also contained a programme, a patch, some badges and a T-shirt. The third Heavy Metal fan was very tall and wore a brand new combat jacket with a Blue Oyster Cult badge on the lapel. Why don't we go and see bands any more? Archie wondered. Like The Undertones, The Buzzcocks (Joy Division backing them up), The Clash, Talking Heads (why did no-one dance till the encore?).

3

Archie recalled with affection: Mental going mental and Davie groovy like a hip rhino.

'You're joking!' shouted the Heavy Metal fan who had asked for the cigarettes. 'The bass player in the support group was absolute garrrr-bage.' Archie and Mental shared a smile at the critique.

The three Heavy Metal fans departed, quietly immersed in themselves. The following day they would tell how 'One guy — real nutter, you know — got dragged away from the big speakers; ears bleeding, the lot. No joking. The bouncers had to drag him away. He had his head stuck right in there. Unbelievable. We got down to row ten. It was great. What was that? My ears are still ringing. And I'll tell you another thing . . .'

Archie sat with his left foot resting on his right knee. His Levi's were well worn, but had seldom been washed. His combat jacket was eight years old. The black boots were as similar to those Springsteen wore on the inner sleeve of *Born in the USA* as you could get for under twenty pounds at the market. A gun-metal grey T-shirt completed his attire. It was baggy at the neck due to squeezing shoulder acne. Archie only squeezed the spots on his shoulders; he left his face alone. For ten years now he had watched his skin deteriorate. The spots seemed to take a lot longer to disappear these days — there was always the same amount but the turnover was not so high. Maybe one day the turnover would stop with the spots turning into moles and you ended up like Leon Brittan. Archie shuddered.

The Mental Kid lit a Marlboro using an expensive looking lighter. Why does he always seem to be starting (never finishing) a cigarette? Archie wondered. I'm always sucking on the filter and he looks as if he's about to get his photograph taken. Maybe I'll tease him about looking like Bowie. That'll get him going. The Kid hated Bowie. A charlatan responsible for the worst clothes and the most sterile music. Mental had been 'smoking Marlboro for years before I knew The Thin White Gook smoked them'. Archie started smoking to look like Bowie. Ten years of tobacco-sponsored cricket, motor-racing and snooker never attracted as many smokers as David Bowie. The Kid had been a Roxy fan (early Roxy,

4

of course) while Archie adored T. Rex. Davie, unfortunately, liked Slade.

Not bothered by the silence, Archie lit up and tried to look like that '77 picture of Bowie. The one in Berlin. Checked shirt and jeans. Lank hair. Mental's cigarette had disappeared.

The anticipation would start up once they got off at Queen Street. That's what happens these days, when we meet up. We all talk at once for ten minutes and we haven't a clue what's been said. Richard called it 'the creation of ignorance through enthusiasm'. Archie was disappointed Richard hadn't come but wasn't surprised.

The train stopped at Lenzie and a pretty, studentish girl got on carrying a paper. It was an *NME* with Bob Dylan and Bob Marley on the front. 'Rockpile '75' Archie could read in the top right-hand corner of the magazine. LPs of the year for 1975. Years ago. That would be interesting. If Richard were here he'd go over and ask to have a look at the paper, thought Archie. He's not got that one. I remember he sent away for it, but couldn't get it. Wonder what number *Born to Run* was? *Horses* (Mental's favourite)? *Young Americans?* (Bowie was smoking on the cover of that.) Why is she reading an old *NME*? Is it hers? I wish I knew people like that. Archie thought about mentioning the girl to Mental but didn't bother. He would definitely tell Richard.

The carriage was littered with commuters' leftovers: discarded tabloids, soft drink cans, crisp packets and cigarette butts. Public transport, private travel. In other circumstances it could have been the remnants of a good time. The only other passenger Archie could see was a tired-looking businessman. The Protestant work ethic.

Another cigarette for Archie. Number 16 for the day. He had an unopened pack of twenty with him just in case there was difficulty in obtaining cigarettes through the night in Glasgow. Archie contemplated picking the mud off his boots and rubbing the muck off his jeans. What the hell, they'll just get dirty again. Oh God; half-senile half-muckpile.

The girl got off at Bishopbriggs and Mental pointed at her paper. 'Did you see that?' he enthused. 'I bet *Horses* beat your *Born to Run*.' Archie now wished he'd pointed out the girl. Mental would have gone over and asked to have a look at the paper. Of course he would. 'Richard's not got that one, eh?' Mental asked. Archie shook his head.

'Welcome to Hun City,' said Archie, pointing to some graffiti outside.

'Fascist bastards! I bet if it was rebel stuff they would have wiped it off.'

The offending words: Rangers, Chelsea, NF.

'Tell me,' said Mental, 'how come an ideologically sound — all that shit — classy player like Pat Nevin plays for those fascists, eh?' Mental was upset. It was like Gerry Adams singing the National Anthem.

'If you were with Clyde and Chelsea offered to sign you up, I think you'd have done the same thing,' said Archie.

'I suppose so,' said Mental but he was still angry. 'Nevin should tell Chelsea to fuck off and come back and play for Celtic. He's a Celtic man. He's not a Hun. He likes good music. Huns like Heavy Metal and George Benson shit.'

'What you havering about, wee shite,' growled Big Davie. His voice was coarse, hard even. Mental claimed it was from singing 'Hello, Hello, We are the Billy Boys' week in week out. Davie, though, said that he never sang sectarian songs and only shouted at individual players. 'Ideologically sound, my arse,' he went on. 'What happened when you played Forest? Viv Anderson got abuse, didn't he? What about that graffiti in Bonnybridge? Celtic and NF in the same paint. Most Celtic supporters link Celtic, IRA, Catholicism and anti-British bigotry. You couldn't even name the six counties , could you?'

'ANTRIM, ARMAGH, DERRY, DOWN, FERMANAGH, TYRONE!' Davie's outburst was a tease to get Mental's back up. The first time Davie asked Mental to name the six counties Mental took five anxious minutes to answer. The Forest game was a deep disgrace and so was the graffiti. Mental wrote to Viv Anderson apologising and blaming infiltrators.

Davie stretched and displayed his massive gut. He farted ostentatiously and said 'Oh, smell that.' Again this was to tease Mental. They had been best friends for fifteen years.

For fifteen years they had talked almost exclusively about football.

Big Davie, satisfied he had teased The Kid enough, lit an Embassy Regal and said, 'Marvin Hagler!'

'Yeah. Marvin Hagler,' said The Mental Kid.

'Marvin Hagler,' said Archie.

'MARR-VIN HAGG-LER,' they chanted, stamping their feet.

The guard entered the carriage and silenced the trio with a finger. 'Hearns'll destroy him,' he said, his face turning into a smile.

'Garrrr-bage. Total and utter garbage,' said The Kid. He looked at his two friends and chanted in a whisper, 'Marrr-vin Hagler.'

Two

'It's raining,' said The Mental Kid. 'Shit.'

'It's not really raining; it's just the wind blowing puddles about,' explained the hydrologically erudite Big Davie.

Mental regarded Davie with suspicion but adjusted his collar (to protect his scarf) and set off. 'Shite!' shrieked the excrementally erudite Mental. 'One of your puddles just fucking soaked me. I'm not going in that. We'll get a taxi. I look wet when it's raining.'

Davie zipped his jerkin up to the neck, adjusted his bunnet and strode off into the rain, laughing at The Kid's protestations.

On a wet and windy night in Glasgow, Archie had no compunction about using the concealed hood of his combat jacket. The full fleshiness of his face shone in the twilight as he pulled tight on the cords. At school, Archie always went bareheaded. He owned a duffel coat which became an object of ridicule. While the body and arms faded to a dirty grey, the hood and shoulders remained navy. Consequently, Archie never used the hood even when it was lashing. So what? West Indian cricketers never wore helmets and they were the best; T. J. Hooker's uniform had no hat and he always caught the bad guys; Mental had never even worn a Celtic tammy. Richard said that statistically hat-wearers were less likely to be involved in road accidents. Hell, that only proved bareheadedness was exciting and dangerous and that hats and hoods were safe and boring.

Archie wanted to stop and light a cigarette. The weather made such a notion ridiculous.

'Hey,' shouted The Kid, 'we're going in here.' The Kid disappeared.

The sign above the doorway was impossible to read, the rain blurring Archie's vision.

'Come on,' said Davie, 'as long as it's not sawdust, shotguns, and *The Wild Rover.*'

They descended a dozen steps then went along a corridor for twenty yards. A woman's voice could be heard to their right. They walked along a bit and came to a split-level bar. Upstairs five student types sat around a table: one male rolling a cigarette, another counting money, the third searching his pockets and saying 'I'm sure I had a fiver when I left. I'm sure. Positive.' Two girls made up the group wondering if the company wasn't just the same as the smalltown creeps they had left behind.

The woman's voice was the barmaid's. She was on the telephone.

Big Davie pointed to a table: a pint of Guinness, a pint of Special, a pint of Carlsberg and six packets of cheese and onion crisps. A black Royal Navy raincoat lay draped over a storage heater. Its owner was playing a slot machine. Davie and Archie sat at the table and supped their drinks. The Kid moved to the jukebox. He shook his head. He shook his head. He shook his head sixteen more times before shaking his fists and shouting 'Yessss.' He inserted his money, selecting Roxy Music's *All I Want Is You.*

'I take it this is where we are,' said Davie to the returning Mental.

'Down 50p,' said Mental referring to his gambling. He sniffed his raincoat. Still wet.

'Anything else on the jukebox?' enquired Archie.

'Just shit.'

9

The three male students eyed the newcomers with suspicion. You couldn't do Richie Benaud impersonations with that racket going on.

The two girls were studying a bottle of pills. 'They're heart pills,' one was saying. 'Gee you up, you know.'

'Is that barmaid talking to Radio Clyde?' asked Davie.

'Some programme about horoscopes. Don't ask me what it's about. I haven't a clue.' The Kid shrugged his shoulders. 'She was on hold when I came in. Her name's Sue. She says we can come back here after the fights. Means we don't have to drink at the poxy Apollo. Thank God. I hate that place. Best guitar solo ever this. None of your Heavy Metal wanking.'

They sat appreciating the music, the drink, the cigarettes and the cheese and onion crisps.

'Still working with that Orange bastard Syme?' Mental asked Davie while disposing of his second crisp packet.

'Yeah, 'fraid so. His patter's all right in small doses but it's the same stories all blooming day. You should hear how he talks about his wife.' Davie shivered as he started his second packet of crisps.

'Mind the day Mad Archie smashed Syme's nose to fuck?' The Kid smiled as if recalling Celtic's finest moment and accepted a grabful of Davie's crisps. Archie smiled modestly.

The cigarette-rolling student was studying the jukebox. He fed money into the machine and started to roll another cigarette. Jeff Beck's *Hi Ho Silver Lining* came booming out the speakers, as subtle as an auntie's kiss.

The four other students groaned, the barmaid groaned and shook her head, Archie groaned and bit his lower lip. Even Davie had had enough of that record.

'I fucking hate that record,' cried Mental. 'I FUCKING HATE IT!'

The student nodded to the beat as he lit his cigarette. The DJ on Radio Clyde could hear the record over the telephone. 'That's a classic,' he said. 'I always play it at the end of my gigs.' '*Really*,' said the barmaid trying not to sound sarcastic.

Good strong beat, thought the student. He had heard the record the other night at a Radio Clyde Roadshow. Maybe he would buy a copy. Had a really strong beat. Good, strong beat.

As he ascended the stairs the others came down.

'We're going,' said one of the girls. 'This place is dead.'

'Fancy coming back to the flat? John said he might be getting some black,' said the cigarette-roller. The two girls looked at each other through dilated pupils and nodded.

As they left, The Kid walked over to the jukebox and extracted the plug. 'Hi Hoooooh . . .' One of the students turned round and said something in a Geordie accent. 'Come on,' said one of the girls in an Angus Og brogue. 'They're not worth bothering about.'

'A gen-u-ine Geordie,' said The Kid. 'Did you see that lassie banging her knee on the heater? See the eyes? Dope city.'

Archie pointed at Big Davie, his hand imitating a gun. He lowered his thumb. Bang!

'The Hun off again. Dearie dear.'

'Anything to save getting his round in,' said Archie. 'Nice place this.'

'All right, I suppose.' Mental lit a cigarette. Archie took one last draw from his. It tasted horrible. Like being stung by lukewarm water. Davie snored, as peaceful and homely as a plate of soup.

Above the bar there was a portable TV. Mental walked over and switched it on. Only two channels were still broadcasting: an Open University class on Furier Series and a black and white French film. In the latter, a woman was cursing a slob in a vest. The woman was very thin and very beautiful. The camera cut to a young girl, cuter than Shirley Temple, playing with limbless teddies and dolls.

'That wee lassie's good at the French,' said Mental.

She had a cheeky face and torn clothes. Cut to woman: torn face and torn clothes, still beautiful.

'What time is it?' asked The Kid.

Archie pointed to a clock at the end of the bar, eyes fixed on the screen.

'Your Mr Simenon's had a tremendous influence on French cinema, eh?' said Mental quoting a half-remembered blurb.

Archie nodded and said, 'Everything's so confined. Nobody ever has more than three good friends,' Archie spoke as if he was unsure of himself, with a shy, jerky voice. Explaining his thoughts, like shaving every day, was something he never really got around to.

'Next thing you'll be complaining about boxing,' joked Mental as Archie stared at the screen.

'I hate the champagne and bow-tie set watching wee boys damage each other. But you can't justify every IRA atrocity, can you?'

Mental nodded and said, 'It's completely different. Boxing can be a bit stupid when it's the heavyweights just leaning on each other. I like the wee guys. All action stuff. Or good guy, bad guy stuff. Like when you beat up Syme and Paul bloody Mercer.'

Paul Mercer was a member of the rugby club and a Bill Beaumont lookalike. One night in the toilet of their local pub, Mercer pushed Archie while Archie was peeing. Archie was furious with embarrassment. He shouted an obscenity at Mercer and a fight ensued. 'Hell hath no fury like a man who is forced to piss himself,' Richard said, explaining why the angrier man won. Thereafter, Richard and Archie had a special friendship. Richard spent his time listening to records, reading books and working in any temporary job he could find. No careers, please. A social and cultural snob, he gave Archie tapes and books and Archie responded with enthusiasm. Archie had never been a 'good laugh' or 'one of the team'; he preferred to play football rather than talk about it, and hated company for the sake of it. Richard was the same. Both were only children.

On the screen the mother and daughter talked. The mother 'explained', the daughter 'listened'. Millions of people and we each get three good friends, thought Archie.

'Marvin Hagler,' said the Celtic supporter.

'Marvin Hagler,' said Archie.

A tear ran down the face of the young French girl. Archie hoped she would get three good friends.

'Cheerio,' said Mental to Sue. He assumed the role of communicator since he was good-looking.

'Enjoy your entertainment, lads.'

'Lads.' That was more like it.

Three

At the Glasgow Apollo, Ran-gers became Rain-bow, stalls substituted terracing, guitar hero for goal scorer, keyboard wizard for midfield maestro, and drum and bass for defence. 'There's only one Ritchie Blackmore . . . Cozy, Cozy, give us a wave.' The Apollo was freezing.

The Apollo also presented boxing nights. Transmissions beamed across the Atlantic in the wee small hours. The ticket prices were high but included a main fight and a supporting bill. Archie had made his mind up a month previous that he would definitely be going. Davie and Mental said it was too expensive. It touched Archie that they had made the effort to save and accompany him on his night out.

The social misfits of all classes and creeds were in attendance: some with pulp science fiction novels protruding from a pocket; journalists hopeless at identifying the support bouts; macho types in casual leather jackets smoking small cigars and exchanging money; shifty types chain-smoking whilst forever removing solid matter from their hair; Scottish pugilists, scrawny kids with balding elders providing motormouth analysis; and the bouncers — bad guys from *Cannon*; moustache, long(ish) hair and flares — for whom there would be no fainting girls to drag out and feel up, and no arrogant pop stars to shove about.

Archie motioned to some central seats about twenty rows back. The Mental Kid wasn't happy so he climbed back five rows to get a better view. Everything's got to suit you, thought Archie with mild annoyance. Calm down, calm down, these seats are better.

The drink, the cold and the excitement made Archie sweat. He and Hagler shared the same birthday — May 23rd. If Isaac Hayes was Black Moses what was there for Hagler? Unappreciated and independent, he was told early in his career to change his attitude and his southpaw stance. The only thing, he was told, that would make him more of an outsider would be to shave his head ... so he shaved his head.

Archie first became aware of Hagler when he took Alan Minter's world title. Minter was alleged to have said 'no black man' would take his title and the fight took place amid an aura of evil-mindedness. The loathsome National Front saw a foothold. When Hagler finished off the brawling Minter he was bombarded with missiles hurled from the crowd. Harry Carpenter was struck as he expressed his shame and fear from the commentary position.

While at school Archie experienced the evil of bigotry. What seemed like the entire male population of St Margaret's turned up to 'claim' Big Davidson, Syme and Loathsome-shit Hunter. (It was known they had humiliated and beaten up two very young Catholic boys.) Archie's school, though, had been dismissed half an hour early. The Catholics were preparing to go home when Archie came shuffling out. He had been detained for persistent lateness. The Catholics raced towards him. Archie ran homeward, but fear made his legs heavy and he was caught easily. Frightened, really frightened, he got pushed against a fence and then to the ground. Kicks, not vicious but persistent, rained in on his body and legs. The pain was secondary to the fear. Like schoolboys de-legging a spider. The spider goes through shit, you know. 'You can give the message,' they said. Archie was sniffling badly, his nose filled with exploding bubbles. He hated Syme and that bunch but he couldn't say anything. Within two minutes the incident was over and the gathering disbanded. Only a smartly dressed kid with a massive Celtic scarf and perfect skin remained. The Mental Kid took Archie home saying, 'I'll always be your best pal. Always.' The Kid demanded his parents place him in a non-denominational school. He hated the nuns, religion, the uniform and the bastard that never picked him for the football team. Loyalty to Glasgow Celtic though came first and Mental remained at St Margaret's. On his return to school Archie was teased for being soft. Big Davidson and Syme stopped him in the corridor. Big Davidson said Archie looked like an ugly girl and Syme pushed Archie making him fall. The world's foremost ideologically-sound fighting machine was born: Mad Archie. Mad Archie punched, kicked and scratched; harder, faster and more often. Syme and Big Davidson both required treatment from the medical officer and Archie got six of the best from a pederast-looking headmaster. Archie was now very unpopular. His best friend was a Catholic and he fought dirty. Beside the school fence and back at the school, Archie had been made to feel that he had done something wrong; that he *was* something wrong. Even Marvin Hagler must have been frightened.

'What time is it?' asked The Mental Kid.

'Time your watch was ready,' said Davie.

'I know. That's three weeks now. I hardly need a watch anyway.'

Davie and Archie gasped. This was the guy who said 'What time is it?' more often than Derek Hatton said 'This Tory government'.

'It's true,' continued The Kid. 'When I was at school, I studied my watch more than the bloody blackboard, you know that. I'm just a little unsettled 'cause we're at the arse end of the day. That's all. See about the watch tomorrow, maybe.'

'Today,' corrected Archie.

'Exactly. Today. Sorry.'

The supporting bouts paired up-and-coming youngsters with old pros carrying debatable records, dependable chins and no history of a big punch. The youngsters were studied concentration. They came, they saw, they gained experience. None caught the eye.

'How you doing, lads?' shouted an old man as he walked up the aisle. Before The Kid could reply, the old man had reached the back of the hall and was ranting to two African students. The old man expressed himself with difficulty. The body's need to cough and splutter coupled with the ill-fitting dentures Charlie Davies loaned him made his attempt at Swahili all the more difficult. The students were from Nigeria, anyway. He understood, though, that they wanted Hearns to win. A lot of the smart money was being placed on Hearns, Archie noted. He had seen Hearns demolish the great Roberto Duran quickly and impressively. American boxing champions seemed especially thin, Milton McCrory was another. Nobody wanted to be a middleweight . . . anything to avoid Marvin Hagler.

Suddenly, everything seemed special. Caesar's Palace was full. The camera panned round the audience. Jack Nicholson! Joan Rivers! A chant went up at the back of the Apollo, 'Tommy Hearns, Tommy Hearns, Tommy Hearns.'

'Marrrr-vin Hag-ler,' screamed The Kid. Davie, Archie and the old man at the back (after removing his dentures) joined the shout for Hagler.

On the screen, the referee told the boxers he wanted a good clean fight. Hearns stood a good few inches taller than Hagler. His hair made him look like a minor league villain in an early seventies blaxploitation flick. One of the guys Shaft beat up then fucked his girlfriend. The fight began.

For Archie, sport was Daley's decathlons, Seb Coe's grace, and Brazilliant football. Archie only had the mildest ambivalence to boxing. He detested the detractors more: the liberals and the racists. Only the skull punches upset him. Body punches and face punches looked great. With athletes the beaten always had a virus; team sports discouraged fitness and personality; tennis, snooker and motor racing pandered to the yuppie mentality, sport as soap opera. Nobody from Castlemilk will ever win Wimbledon. Boxing was different. Ali, Leonard, Hagler, Duran; stick that in your personal computer and the printout reads 'No bullshit'.

Hagler and Hearns were at fucking war. Hagler aggressive, Hearns alert and accurate. Nobody offered to score round one. Caesar's Palace, Las Vegas and The Apollo,

Glasgow breathed the same breath. A declaration of war interrupting the broadcast would have caused a riot.

Round two. The same, only more so. 'He's cut. Hagler's cut,' came the shout from the back of the hall. 'Tommy Hearns, Tommy Hearns, Tommy Hearns,' Archie was crying and screaming, 'Get him. GET HIM!!!'

Round three. Cut and troubled? Facing defeat? Losing? On the contrary Marvin Hagler seemed quite taken by the prospect. Hearns knew it would take all his courage, strength, experience and skill to keep Hagler at bay. Hagler waded in, Hearns stood his ground . . . he shouldn't have. PUNCH! PUNCH! His legs turned to jelly and he had an incredible desire to lie on the floor. The fight was over and Marvellous Marvin Hagler remained the Undisputed Middleweight Champion of the World. No sweat, like.

The three friends slapped palms and hugged each other. This was a night they would recall for the rest of their lives. Mental wore Davie's bunnet leaving the latter bald. Everything was great. Wonderful. Macho bullshit, maybe, but wonderful.

After the interviews they left. Everybody said the same two words: 'Marvin Hagler'. They were all smiling and they were all friends.

Outside dawn had broken. The pleasure spoiled by the smell of discarded takeaways.

Archie was pleased it was his initiative that located the pub. Mental thought it was the other way.

'You're back,' said Sue. She was checking all the bingo in all the papers. 'Cross, cross, cross . . . shit, shit, shit. Got some rolls made up for you. Okay?'

'Magic,' said The Mental Kid, the Egon Ronay rating he accorded all food apart from square sausages, eggs and cauliflowers.

They ate and drank heartily, replenishing the sweat loss with zest. Mental thanked Sue and told her she'd been more than kind.

Half an hour and a quick two pints later, Mental was drunk. Happy drunk.

'She's good looking, Sue, eh?' he said. 'You know I used to keep a top ten chart of the most desirable women.'

Mental paused to burp. 'I called it the Mental Top Ten. Geddit? In my head, mental; and me, Mental. A pun, like.' Davie and Archie nodded that they understood. 'Anyway,' continued The Kid, 'Sue would be a new entry, she would.'

'Out of interest,' said Davie, 'did my intended ever figure in this chart of yours?'

'Of course. Terasa is a very beautiful woman!'

'How about blue-and-yellow?' asked Archie.

The Kid looked over his left shoulder, over his right shoulder, and under the table. He put his hand atop his mouth and said, 'Number One for eighty-seven weeks.' Archie and Davie were impressed. Blue-and-yellow used to live across the road from Mental and was in Archie and Davie's year at school. The name derived from a dress she used to wear. She had always been beautiful but with that dress on . . . They always looked for blue-and-yellow to wear the dress again, but she never did. It hadn't been seen for two years.

'You know what upset the chart?' asked Mental. Archie shrugged. 'Haircuts,' announced Mental. 'Young girls get the most stupid haircuts.'

'Hippies look good when they get their hair cut,' said Archie.

'Hey, don't get me wrong, I hate hippies as much as the next man, but you've got to remember that haircut blue-and-yellow got.'

Archie remembered. She was in his Modern Studies class at the time. The teacher laughed at her and blue-and-yellow started crying and went home. Archie wanted to kill the teacher. The haircut looked bloody awful, though.

'See what I mean.' Mental was triumphant. 'A haircut is a haircut, you're just getting your hair cut. Is that Hun sleeping again? Dearie dear.' Mental tutted and lay on the floor. He didn't think he could fall off that.

Mental dreamt of Sue. His hands caressing her legs, rubbing and stroking. But the little black patterns on her tights started moving: over his arms, legs and face; into his ears, mouth and eyes. Faster and faster. Mental grabbed and stroked at thin air. Sue laughed at him. As Mental licked and kissed, his skin was burning and his vision blurring. Lust and anxiety became one.

'Hey you,' shouted Big Davie. 'Come on. Time for the train. Having one of your Catholic guilt dreams again?'

'You don't know what it's like. You'll never know.' Mental held his scarf to his chest; an umbilical cord.

''Bye Sue,' said Mental as they left. 'You've been very good to us.'

'That's okay. I had some good fun while you were asleep.' Sue winked enigmatically as Archie brushed his hand over the zip of his trousers and Mental screamed inside.

During the journey home Davie talked of his day ahead: work, the people, the boredom. Davie was a fearful man when he was pissed off: increasingly sullen and crude. He had always found it easy to get along, always been easy-going, but now he sounded bitter about life. Scunnered. Terasa worked in an office where he knew none of the people and any mention of them resulted in nervous jealousy . . . and he, Davie, worked with a collection of rejects. Richard told him to jack the job in if it upset him so much. Go for a walk, read a book, see some friends. But Davie wasn't like that.

The train arrived home at the back of seven. Davie bought his supplies for the day: a *Daily Record*, a bottle of Irn Bru and two packets of cheese and onion crisps.

'Going out tonight?' shouted Mental as Davie headed for the council workshops.

'No. Not tonight.'

'Okay, we'll be round for the boxing then.'

'Right, see you.'

'See you,' said Archie.

'So this is seven o'clock in the morning, eh?' Mental said as he and Archie walked home. 'Seven o'clock in the morning. People do this every bloody day, you know. Look at them. Waiting on buses, waiting on trains. Seven o'clock in the morning, all Hell chained up. I was at school with that guy. Haven't seen him for years. God, he looks about fifty! Christ! Fuck this shit. Half-nine, that's the time to get up. I can't handle these people.'

Mental had a good slag for most everyone they met: a boilersuited lad with a Rangers scarf ('Orange bastard'), the factory girls ('They are *so* thick'), a guy with a Hearts scarf ('I hate Hearts more than I hate Rangers'), Asian shop-keepers ('How come they never smile?'), students ('Never met one with integrity yet').

'I mean,' summed up Mental, 'do these people actually think they look good when they look in the mirror? Could you tell me?'

As they arrived at Mental's block of flats they met Mental's dad (a dead ringer for Bobby Lennox) walking the golden labrador Jinky. Archie liked Mental's dad. He worked in Daz Island — a wee while on, a wee while off. Theirs was the only proper family in the block. Although they could have afforded to stay in a private house they chose to remain where they were happy. Because of his father's wealth, Mental reasoned he didn't have to pay dig money — so he didn't. Mental was spoilt rotten. His father paid for the ticket to the boxing.

'Good night, was it?' Mental's dad asked Archie.

'Magic. How you doing, Jinky? Celtic paw, Rangers paw, Celtic paw, Rangers paw, Celtic paw, Celtic paw.' The dog obligingly lifted its front paws, Celtic being a left-footer.

'See you later,' said Archie. 'I'm knackered.'

'Yeah. I'll give you a phone and we'll go over the town and see about my watch.'

'Okay,' said Archie. 'Be good.'

When Archie got home, his father had already left for work. His mother was still in bed. Archie went straight to his room. He changed into an old Levi's sweatshirt and a pair of Adidas shorts. The boxing trip had been Archie's idea and it had been a great success. Archie felt proud but he realised that these outings were now a thing of the past. A smile straightened his lips as the poster on the wall came into focus. 'Marvin Hagler,' he said aloud. 'Marvin fucking Hagler!'

Back at the Apollo the old man searched joylessly for his dentures. Oh well, he decided, I'll just need to get another pair. A better fit this time.

Four

Archie slept well. He rose at ten past two. Normally his body felt stiff and sore, and his mind would be confused. For a while there he'd been plagued by the recurring question 'Who played right back for The Clash?' For a few seconds he would worry about this then suffer a dull depression when it dawned on him that he would never know. But today was different. The boxing had removed a lot of tension. He did his exercises: a hundred hurried but perfect press-ups, a hundred sit-ups and a hundred deep knee-bends. His stomach was solid. His arms, however, lacked the same firmness — although they looked powerful when he folded them across his chest. Need to find out about developing my upper body, Archie told himself for the millionth time. He would never use organised facilities for training. He had never in his life joined a boys' club, youth club or any other organisation. Archie tried to join a local junior football side when he was eleven. He was pelted with stones, rocks, clay and shale. He had bought a brand new pair of football boots in anticipation of the occasional game. (He knew he was better than some of the boys that played.) Crying, Archie ran home. He sobbed and sniffled all night. His father protested and Archie was invited along the following Tuesday, assured he would get the chance to prove himself. He didn't go. The singer Bill Withers had joked, 'It ain't the being shot at, it's the being shot!' but being shot at was enough for Archie. Joining a club was like looking through somebody's photographs or going into somebody's house. It was an invasion of intimacy. Nobody ever apologised to Archie for the incident. Nobody even mentioned it. And his mother never got to wash a team of football strips.

Archie lit a cigarette and alternated puffs with the dressing ritual. The first cigarette was always the best of the day. Having one before brushing his teeth meant he had this pleasure twice. I'll change the sheets tomorrow, he told himself after arranging the bedclothes in a perfunctory manner.

In the bathroom he washed his face and brushed his teeth. He couldn't be bothered shaving. A cluster of spots on his right cheek marred his complexion.

'Soup in pot' read the note from his mum. As the soup heated Archie made himself two raspberry jam pieces and poured himself a glass of milk. He stirred the soup. Pea and ham. The phone rang.

'Ibrox Stadium. Can I help you?' said Archie as he lifted the receiver.

'Hi. Still coming round?' said The Mental Kid. 'Did you sleep all right?'

'Yeah, I'm just fixing some dinner.'

'I was going to make something but I can't be bothered. Feel all right, like, just don't feel hungry.' His dreams had been upset by patterned tights.

'Nobody to make it for you, you mean. You're helpless, you know that?'

'Come off it. I can look after myself. I may be a parasite but I'm not helpless. I don't hide behind my mother's skirts. I think things through, you know.'

'I'll need to watch my soup. See you about three, okay.'

'Okay, see you.'

The soup was starting to boil. Archie lifted the pot off the ring and poured the soup into a big dish. He rinsed the pot and left it in the basin. Half past two. His mother would be home from her school dinners job at three by which time Archie would be gone.

The soup, pieces and milk quickly devoured, Archie washed the dishes in boiling water with a generous squirt of the scented washing-up liquid. He let his hands steep in the basin. Masochistic bullshit. Ahhhhhh. Remembering to dry off the pot with the cloth before applying the dishtowel and wipe some jam off the table, he finished in the kitchen. He added 'See you later, crocodile' to the note then returned to his room.

Archie got on well with his parents until the subjects of marriage and employment were raised, making Archie blush and get angry. It was always uncles and aunts that wanted to know. It was all they had to ask him. They were astonished that Archie was qualified for university. If sixth year, though, was a taster then Archie wanted none of it. Addressing teachers by their first names and all that handshaking; it was like being accepted by Christians.

'I am the son and heir of a shyness that is criminally vulgar,' sang Morrissey while Archie put on his combat jacket and boots. Always play a good record before you leave home, Richard said. And it was good advice. It was great to walk down the street with The Smiths in your head. Once Archie had left for school and the last record he heard on the radio was Lynsey de Paul's *Sugar Me*. Archie couldn't get the song out of his head all day. It hurt and nauseated him. Never again.

He left through the back door of the terraced flat and out between two rows of garages. Large holes appeared on the walls of the flats where the rough-cast had fallen off. Any more and the buildings would start to look like England's redbrick land. The council said it would repair the damage come summer and the better weather. And they would.

Buzzzzzzz. Archie pressed the button next to No. 116.

The Mental Kid was wearing the late Tam Wilson's best suit, which Mental had bought at Barnardo's for two pounds. He hadn't realised it was old Tam's suit when he bought it. It wouldn't have mattered anyway. 'The suit is smart. Somebody would have bought it, so why not me?' Old Tam's wife still lived across the road. Mental also wore a cream shirt and a burgundy tie. A pair of Raybans rested on his nose.

'Pretty smart, eh?' said The Kid, indicating the glasses.

'When did you get them?'

'They're Kelly's.' The Kid's twin sister. 'Five ninety-nine out that record shop up Logie Baird Drive. Bit tight, though, and I can't see a thing.'

They looked like a couple of clumsy and callous hitmen. The Kid Clu Gulager in *The Killers* and Archie skinny and scruffy like De Niro in *Taxi Driver*.

'Some night, eh?' said Archie.

'Seems unreal. Especially that pub. Does that place ever close? I was glad to get to my bed, though.'

'Wonder how Davie got on at work?'

'He'll be all right. I wouldn't sleep anywhere near that lot. I've an idea of what they would do, especially Syme.' Mental sucked air but added nothing.

'There's a lot worse than Syme in the world,' said Archie as they entered the park.

'I don't disagree. I mean people who molest children every day are worse than those who only do it at weekends. But they're still bastards.'

Had Archie been on his own he would have walked through the football pitches regardless of the mud. The Mental Kid, however, had never traversed a puddle let alone mud. Consequently, they took the long route round the path, encountering overalled council workers on their way. Trainees with transistors, supervisors with clipboards and ties. One 'must be under 24' the other 'must be 24+'. Steve Wright a grating offence on the radio.

'How can you skive off a job where you do nothing, eh?' Mental knew the workers by sight and footballing loyalty. 'They wait for it to rain so they can go indoors and play cards. Dearie dear.'

'What they do/they smile in your face/all the time they wanna take your place/The Backstabbers.' The O'Jays' classic was interrupted by Mr Wright being 'amusing'. Lord Reith spun and spun.

'See that. He plays a decent record and he fucking interrupts it. That guy is the ultimate prick.' The council workers looked on in bemusement. Why did this guy have to get so worked up? Mental was passionate about everything: from cauliflowers to nuclear wars. If he upset people, all the better.

A group of schoolchildren ran across the park singing 'Here we go, here we go, here we go.' Some had sports bags, some had carrier bags, and some just had towels. They were returning to school after a visit to the baths.

Mental shook his head and said, 'Typical Scottish mentality, singing that song. Scots sing that the same way Huns sing "Hello, Hello, We are the Billy Boys". That's *all* they ever sing.' Archie pointed to two at the back. Neither running nor singing, they were smoking, though.

'The Huns, obviously,' said Mental. 'They can't remember the words. I bet they can't read or write. Any money? Did you see that thing on *Newsnight*? There were these guys and they could do nothing: reading, writing, sums, nothing. I'm intelligent, right? And when I left school I couldn't do fractions. And do you know why? Because nobody bothered their backside.'

'Hey, look over there!' shouted Archie enthusiastically.

'DOSTOYEVSKY!' yelled The Kid aiming for a seismograph reading.

Dostoyevsky was that rarity of rarities: intelligent, a vegan, fun-loving, domesticated . . . and a Dobermann pinscher. Richard Pryor said that the Dobermann looked as if it spent the best part of its life being abused. And while it's true most Dobermanns look like the canine equivalent of Glasgow Rangers supporters — vicious, thick and ugly — this one had grace and style. His coat shone like a jazzman's trumpet, his eyes were as keen as a child's, and his frame was as graceful and athletic as that of Carl Lewis.

The Mental Kid had traces of canine odour upon his person, and as well as greeting his Catholic friend, Dostoyevsky wanted a good sniff.

'Hey, get off you. That's the serious shit down there.' Mental adopted his I-am-superior-to-dogs voice and aimed a manly get-your-nose-away-from-my-willy swipe.

'Dostoyevsky, where's Richard?' asked Archie. The dog stopped sniffing and did his impression of a pointer.

26

Archie followed the dog's gaze. A figure approached; incredibly skinny with a big smile. Richard wore white Levi's and a Levi jacket, a T-shirt advertising Defunct, and a pair of ten-year-old black gym shoes. His hair was thick, blond and greasy. He claimed to look like a cross between Lee Perry and Laura Nyro. Davie, though, said that Richard looked like an extra from *Fame*, offensively happy and skinny.

'What are you doing to my dog, you?' Richard asked Mental.

'Okay, so Catholics shag dogs. Let's all have a good laugh,' moaned Mental.

'What you been up to?' asked Archie. 'Not seen you for a while.'

'Yeah. Well, I finished up at the Italian restaurant on Sunday there, so you'll probably be seeing a bit more of me over the next few weeks.' Archie was pleased. Richard's voice was as accentless as Scots gets, a product of reading (which he did a lot of) as opposed to speaking (which he did little of). Richard generally used his intelligence to start conversations and let others relate the anecdotes and opinions. In one-to-one situations, however, he talked non-stop. Most days he just spent listening to records, going for walks and reading books and magazines. Richard owned more records than Archie had ever seen and had a cupboardful of old music papers and fanzines, all read and all treasured.

The previous summer, Richard had been dumped by his girlfriend of three years standing, Susan Jones. Richard turned totally in on himself: he listened to nothing but Howlin' Wolf records for a fortnight, became a vegan, bought a Dobermann and took any work that was going — eighteen-hour shifts, working with shite, anything. His goal eventually was to own a record shop. Together, he and Susan did crosswords, watched soap operas and quiz shows, cooked and contributed to late-night phone-ins. Archie and Richard became friends because of their exclusion from the conversations about football. Richard had previously gone out with Mental's big sister. He was a year older than Archie, but he would always look like a happy nineteen-year-old. Mention of Susan Jones still caused Richard to blush and reported sightings resulted in nervous aggression.

'Have you signed on?' asked Mental.

'Never signed off,' replied Richard smugly.

'Dearie dear, and you with all your millions stashed away. You must be loaded, eh?' Mental always teased Richard about his wealth. Richard never denied he saved money. He was also sole heir to his elderly parents' detached villa, their BMW and their personal wealth. Including the value of his records and papers, Richard was worth a lot of money.

They headed towards the town. Archie wanted to tell Richard about the girl with the *NME,* the fight, the Simenon novel he was reading (*The Iron Staircase*) and the Tim Buckley and Nick Drake tapes Richard had given him. Mental, though, was already relating the previous night's events: the girl with the *NME* (Richard had just got a copy of that through the post. *Born to Run* wasn't in the LPs of the year. Archie was stunned), the fight (Richard knew the result) and the *Hi Ho Silver Lining* torture (he was particularly sympathetic to this). Archie was pleased that Mental spoke of the previous night's events. It meant he'd had a good time. Archie was not a story-teller. He would have found it easier to spell diarrhoea backwards. He would have found it easier to *do* diarrhoea backwards.

At the edge of the park, Richard stopped and put Dostoyevsky's lead on.

'Hey, watch this,' said The Kid and stamped his foot on the zebra crossing causing three cars to brake sharply.

'I hate motorists as much as you do, Mental. But . . .' Richard left the sentence hanging. There was little point in chastising The Kid, there seldom was. As he said, he thought things through.

One of the drivers rolled down his window and swore at The Kid. The 'fucking prick', however, was checking his appearance in the window of a parked car.

They arrived at the main shopping precinct and Richard secured Dostoyevsky to a tree. 'No barking. No shitting,' he instructed. 'If anybody hassles you just give them the stare.'

Dostoyevsky adopted his anybody-want-a-staring-match pose. Richard Pryor said that Dobermanns 'hypnotise your ass' when they stare at you. The anatomy boggles.

'I can't see a thing in here,' said Mental once they were in the jewellers.

'Well, take them off,' suggested Archie.

'No. Everybody'll see the red marks at the side of my nose.'

'Everybody' was a young couple buying an engagement ring (Him: 'It's a bit expensive.' Her: 'But it is lovely, though') and the assistant attending them.

Archie felt confident and pressed a button marked *Ring for service*. It was a loud bell.

'There will be somebody to see you presently, sir,' said the assistant in a voice he normally reserved for rebuking his grandchildren. Archie smiled coyly and scuffed his feet off the floor. He decided not to get upset at being called 'sir'. The guy was probably expected to use a mode of address. Part of the job, like.

'Sorry to have kept you waiting. What can I do for you?' The woman emerged from the workshop wearing a plain black skirt and a white blouse. The outline of her bra was clearly visible including the detail on the breasts. Archie never knew whether he was supposed to find this sexy. It seemed silly to him. Her hair was lavish and framelike in the manner of a newsreader.

'My watch?' said Mental.

'Your name, please?'

Mental gave his name.

'And you handed it in three weeks ago?'

'A-ha.'

She went back into the workshop and returned with the watch.

'It just needed new batteries. If you'd have waited when you handed it in we could have done it for you at the time. Two pounds, please.' The woman spoke to Mental as if he were very silly.

'What time is it?' Archie asked The Kid once they were outside reversing the comment he had heard non-stop for the past three weeks.

29

'I don't know, I can't see the display with these glasses on.' Archie was deflated and left to wonder if The Kid would ever see himself as others saw him.

While they were in the shop, Dostoyevsky had outstared two pensioners, five skinheads, an Alsatian and an Irish wolfhound. He was currently working on two Yorkshire terriers. He imagined them revolving on a spit, greasy and fatty. *Just put them in a microwave for five minutes and I'll clean up the mess.*

'No, you can't eat them. You're a vegan,' said Richard.

'What did you have for dinner, Dostoyevsky?' asked Archie.

Baked potatoes. They were okay. They looked like cat's brains. Made a change from beetroot, though. I've ate more beetroot than Poland.

The Yorkies were showing signs of derangement. They bounced as they barked, as though they'd just swallowed scorpions.

'What is *that*?' cried The Kid.

'That's that new guy, William Stevenson. They call him Tesco — he stores food, geddit? He's moved into one of those flats across the road from me — McGonnigal Drive — with his wife.' Richard indicated a frail looking girl in a brown skirt and a white T-shirt. 'Guess how old he is?'

Archie looked at Tesco: six foot four, fifteen stone, balding, sports top, beige cords, forearms and neck tattooed.

'He's eighteen!' said Richard.

'*Eight-een*,' repeated The Kid. 'Not on this planet he's not. Mother Nature's fucked up there. Grade-A psycho-hun.'

'Poor guy,' said Archie.

'What do you mean "poor guy"?' cried Mental. 'People like him should ... I don't know. Just look at him, for God's sake.' The Kid looked agitated, like a cat in the rain. Orangemen had hate in the pores of their skin and on the retinas of their eyes. He would joke about 'the Huns': how thick and ugly they were, but the reality was no joke.

Tesco pushed his wife and she stumbled forward. Dostoyevsky could spot a fascist bastard at half a mile; he barked fiercely and pulled on his lead.

'Go on Dostoyevsky. Kill him. I'll give you fifty quid if you kill him,' said Mental.

Tesco looked over in the direction of the barking. Saliva filled Archie's mouth but he could not swallow. He was frightened. He shivered.

'I bought some shit off Wee Stevie this morning. Fancy coming round for a smoke later on?' said Richard, changing the subject.

'I'm into that,' enthused Mental. 'We're going round to Davie's to watch the boxing at eight.'

'Davie come up too?'

'Suppose so,' said Mental. 'Terasa won't though.'

'I'll need to get some skins,' said Richard and they headed off to *Menzies*.

Dostoyevsky got tied to a tree. He sniffed at the canine excrement that lay there. *Interesting, very interesting.*

Inside *Menzies*, Archie picked up a copy of *Boxing News* and Richard studied *Rolling Stone*.

'Five stars for that!' shrieked Mental looking at *Sounds*. 'They must be joking.'

'Excuse me. I said excuse me. You're fine and tall.'

Richard looked round then down. The frail, old voice came from a frail, old woman. Sadly, she had never reached five feet.

'You're fine and tall. Could you reach up and get me that copy of *Vogue*. Thank you very much. My, you're fine and tall. That's very good of you.' She looked at the magazine for a few seconds then said, 'No, that's last month's. Is there not another one there?'

'No.'

'Are you sure, son?' Richard shook his head. 'Oh well,' said the old woman. 'Thanks anyway. You're fine and tall.'

'I'm only five foot ten,' said Richard but she was off. Richard walked over to the counter and said, 'Two packets of cigarette papers, please. The red ones, please.'

Archie wondered if the amount of shit smoked was estimated by comparing the amount of hand-rolling tobacco sold with the amount of cigarette papers sold. Only a few students and old-timers used loose tobacco. What would the unions and management at Rizla think of this?

31

'What time is it?' asked The Kid as Richard untied Dostoyevsky.

'*Countdown* time,' said Richard.

'I hate that programme,' said Mental. 'Full of boring bastards.'

'*Countdown*'s the only quiz programme I watch,' said Richard. 'It's not like Jimmy Tarbuck or Les Dawson.'

'I beat you that time we watched *Countdown*,' said Archie to The Kid.

'Sure. Sure,' said The Kid. 'A stupid wee game. I'm hopeless at anything like that. It takes a certain kind of mentality to be good at these programmes. The sort of mentality that likes American football, kitchen units and George Benson. There's Margaret Bannon, I got my first inside feel off her.' Mental smiled at her. She smiled back.

Dostoyevsky was pulling Richard towards a rogue shopping trolley.

'Come on,' said Richard. 'You can't eat it and you can't have sex with it.'

I can smell meat: liver, kidneys, steak, sausages. Oh, fuck it. Beetroot, here we come.

They walked homeward, comfortable in the company.

'I'll tape the boxing so you can see it again,' said Richard as he entered his block of flats.

'See you later,' said The Kid and Archie together. 'The back of nine it'll be,' added The Kid.

Five

'That guy Tesco upset me,' said The Kid. 'Did you see him? That's just what this town needs. An arsehole like that. I know the IRA are a bit out of order at times — not so much recently, though — but they still base their philosophy on intelligence not dogma. Those Orange bastards haven't a clue. They're just bigots.'

'A lot of your Celtic friends are equally bigoted. It's all this "I support the armed struggle" romanticism. It's all about God and country. Two things which neither of us could care less about.'

'The IRA has nothing to do with Catholicism. Ireland is a very conservative country. Sinn Fein is a socialist party remember.'

'I'm just saying that some of your friends hate Orangemen for the same reasons they hate you.'

'No. Wrong. We hate all Orangemen, not all Protestants. They hate all Catholics. There's a big difference, there.'

They had reached Mental's flat.

'Pop round later. Back of six.'

'Okay,' said Archie. 'Be good.'

Archie reached home at quarter to five. His father was studying the television page of the *Daily Record*. His mother

33

could be heard singing in the kitchen. Archie went to his room and played The Undertones' *You've Got My Number* (Brilliant!) and *Let's Talk About Girls* (Awesome!) while taking his boots and jacket off. He lit a cigarette and wondered who M. Freiser, the composer of the latter, was.

'Tea-time,' shouted Archie's mum. Archie went through to the kitchen with the riff from *Let's Talk About Girls* pounding in his head. Great!

They had potatoes, stewed steak, Brussels sprouts and apple crumble (Archie's favourite) for tea. Archie asked his parents how work had been. Nothing new, they reported. If he had asked more specific questions maybe they would have elaborated more, but he couldn't think of anything to ask so he told them about his night out. Archie had more confidence talking about his friends as he got older. Previously he had been shy at mentioning Davie, Mental and Richard; but now he was proud. They were a lot better than that crowd of weirdo relations he had been dragged around as a child. Archie was more thoughtful in front of his parents since he started reading Simenon. Fewer of his sentences ended in three dots. He used clarity rather than vocabulary to impress them. He related the events with controlled enthusiasm to emphasise he was happy.

Archie's relationship with his parents had not changed as he got older. He could have been fourteen or, he supposed, forty. His father once said: 'Don't criticise me, you haven't earned the right.' But Archie suspected he never would earn the right. He tried to impress his father by memorising handyman tips (grease all moving parts, etc.) and facts about relations. These things, though, were the products of experience and Archie was no nearer to owning a tool kit than the day he was born.

After tea, they sat down and watched the *News at 5.45*. There was a bit about the fight at the end.

Archie went through to his room and read a chapter of *The Iron Staircase*. He smoked a cigarette while getting ready to go out and listening to a 12" of The Heptones' *Good Life*. The homeliness of the lyrics made him feel a bit sad and selfish. This was a part of him that Archie didn't like thinking about too much. He played

Let's Talk About Girls again to cheer himself up. What a record!

'I'm away to see The Kid.' Archie stuck his head in the living-room door. His parents were watching *Scotland Today*. 'Then we're going to see Davie and Terasa then Richard.' Archie enjoyed mentioning Terasa's name. He wasn't sure why. It wasn't just because she was a girl.

'Okay, son,' said Archie's mum. 'We're thinking of taking a run through to see your Aunt Isabel so mind and take your key.'

'What time's the boxing on?' said Archie's dad.

'Eight o'clock.' Why did he ask that? He's got the paper in front of him.

'So it is.'

Archie's mother went over to the unit and removed the telephone address book. A piece of paper fell out. It was the piece of paper she used to note down the names and addresses of any neighbours she came across while browsing through the telephone book.

'I'll phone Isabel just now,' said Archie's mother while Archie's father set up the video to record the boxing.

'Cheerio,' said Archie. I wonder when they decided to go out? They never mentioned it at tea-time.

'Cheerio,' said his mum. 'Mind your key.'

The fresh evening air brought a chill to his cheeks. He was glad to have passed another day without any hassle about jobs.

Buzzzzzz. 'Yeah,' said a girl's voice.

'Pat Nevin,' said Archie into the entryphone and he pushed the door open. The sound of jangly guitars increased as Archie climbed the stairs. REM, decided Archie . . . *Pretty Persuasion*.

The door to Mental's flat lay open and Archie let himself in. The first door on the left had a picture of the current Celtic team on it. Archie gave the door a tuneful tap and entered.

Mental was lying on the bed completing the tracklisting of a cassette inlay card. A tricolour served as a bedspread. Mental smiled and said, 'Just taping these records.' He lowered the volume from four to two. 'You got *Reckoning*?'

'Yeah, it's great. What's your favourite track?'

'Eh, let me think. I prefer the second side.' Mental studied the inlay card. '*Camera*, I suppose. A bit obvious.'

'What other records did Richard give you?'

'Ehhhhhh . . . ahhhh. *Veedon Fleece*, which is surprisingly excellent, and . . . oh yeah, *Clear Spot*, which is miles better than *Trout Mask* . . . any day.'

'*Clear Spot*'s awesome. The third best LP of all time,' said Archie with a smile on his face. Mental smiled his no-it-isn't smile.

How could people get so worked up about relatives and cars when there were records? Records cut so much deeper. For Mental, *Astral Weeks, Closer* and *For Your Pleasure* (the three best LPs of all time, he said. No contest) articulated the mundanity, despair and joy of existence. For Archie, it was the exuberance of classic Motown, T. Rex and (to the surprise of a lot of people) Prince. Prince made God look like a prototype. Mental said his records were the most important things in his life — more important than Celtic, easily. It's just that football was easier to talk about for five hours down the pub on a Saturday night.

The Kid descended from his bunk gingerly and turned the record over. He surveyed the recording process and said, 'Okay. Do you want to see my dad's new ship?'

'Another one?'

'It's not finished yet. But it's starting to take shape.'

Mental turned the volume down to zero and they went through to the living-room.

There were photographs all over the living-room. All the family and friends. At home, Archie's parents had no photographs on show. All the photographs were in a couple of shoeboxes; mostly black and white. Mental's living-room was a homely mess; papers, books, envelopes, ashtrays lay everywhere. Aristotle said that some men were born leaders and, by implication, that some men were born slaves. Mental's family were born to be visited and Archie's were born visitors. Archie could never understand how his relatives never 'phoned or popped in. It was always Archie's parents who instigated a meeting. In Mental's home, neighbours, friends and family popped in all the time.

'That you admiring my latest masterpiece?' said Mental's dad. He was smoking a pipe and knotting a scarf around his neck. He was wiry, affable and proud as hell he looked like Bobby Lennox. When he was home he ran the local Celtic supporters' club and collected for the miners. 'It's shaping up better than the first one. More stable looking.' The boat would eventually be suitable for sailing down the park. He would maybe sell it.

Archie didn't know what to say so he just relied on self-deprecation. 'I'm hopeless at anything to do with my hands.'

'Anyway,' said Mental's dad, 'we're away. Where's your lead, Jinky?'

'Take a slice of that,' said Mental, handing Archie a slice of sponge. Archie accepted. It was the lightest sponge he had ever tasted.

'I think he likes it,' said Mental.

'You'd better tell him it's a fiver a slice,' shouted Mental's mum from the kitchen.

Kelly, Mental's twin sister, appeared. 'I smell baking,' she said and made a beeline for the kitchen. She worked in a travel agent's over the town. 'By the way, Archie,' she added. 'It's Brian McClair I've got the hots for these days.' Mental and Mental's mum looked on in bewilderment as Archie and Kelly shared a smile.

'I'll have to bake another cake now. That one was for Joyce. She said she would pop round later,' sighed Mental's mum.

'None of your Scottish muck in this house,' said Mental. 'What did you have for your tea? Mince and tatties, I suppose.'

'Chilli con carne,' lied Archie, who didn't even know what chilli con carne was.

'You're a liar, Scottish food makes you fat, ugly and gives you heart attacks. We had . . .'

Three interlopers were in the bedroom.

'What you doing?' said Mental.

'Nothing. I haven't done nothing,' said Paddy, Mental's fourteen-year-old nephew. His domestic situation wasn't very stable and he spent most of his time at Mental's.

Mental surveyed the recording process. 'You better not have,' he said. Everything seemed okay.

'This is Tim Craig, Roy's wee brother, and Charlie Nicholas, no relation of course,' said Paddy introducing his friends.

'Is that your real name?' Mental was impressed. The painfully thin redhead nodded. 'I think I've seen you on the bus a few times. Never knew that was your name. Pretty smart.'

There was a poster of the other Charlie Nicholas on the wall as well as pictures and souvenirs of other Celtic legends: Jimmy Johnstone, nine-in-a-row, Kenny Dalglish and Vic Davidson (what ever happened to Vic Davidson?), European Cup Final, Mo Johnston and Brian McClair. There was a poster of V. I. Lenin and one quoting the words of Bobby Sands, 'You can put a rope around a man but you can't put a rope around an idea.' There was a video compilation of Celtic's great moments: Mental in the crowd at Hampden (there were ten thousand people in the frame but you could still identify him), a Celtic player clearly mouthing the words 'Fuck off, ya Orange bastard' at the referee, the classic goals and the great games all carefully edited by Mental's dad. Archie took his cigarettes out and lit one. He picked up a copy of *Republican News* and studied it as if he were at the dentist.

'Any chance of crashing some fags?' asked Paddy.

'If you're going to smoke, you can buy your own,' said Mental, half-brother half-bastard.

Archie found an ashtray on the window ledge and placed it on top of a speaker. 'What you doing tonight?' Archie asked Paddy.

'Don't know, going out, I suppose. Just going out.' Paddy and his two friends sat on the bed. Their timidity belied their reputation.

'Well, this record's nearly finished so we're going out,' explained Mental, 'and I'm not having you three in here ruining my system so you're going out too.' Mental was harsh. He didn't like Roy Craig and if Paddy was palling around with that family . . .

'Come on. Let's go,' said Paddy.

'See you, lads,' said Archie. The Kid said nothing.

'I see you lost the red marks on your nose.'

'They were pretty bad. I've got some make-up on. You couldn't walk about with marks like that.'

'Never,' agreed Archie, trying to sound sarcastic, although he would have done the same.

The music stopped. The Kid took the record off the turntable and placed it in the inner sleeve then placed the inner sleeve in the record cover. While Mental searched out *Veedon Fleece* and *Clear Spot*, Archie wound the tape to the end, then removed it and put it in its box. He positioned the box in the inverted pelmet which served as a container for Mental's cassettes next to a couple of rebel tapes — *Teddy Bears' Picnic* and *Revolutionary Songs*. Boxcar Willie with shamrocks, Richard called them. They're quite good, some of them, said Mental. Especially when you're wrecked.

'"Jefferson, I think we're winning",' sang The Kid and selected a baggy cream cardigan from his wardrobe. He straightened his tie, then loosened it before putting on a massive wool overcoat. A quick check in the mirror. Loosen the tie a bit more. Okay.

'Let's shoot,' said Mental. 'The cardie's a bit big but it's cold outside.'

Archie nodded and extinguished his cigarette.

'Cheerio. I'll be late,' shouted Mental to no one in particular, carrying the records businesslike, underarm, in a *Menzies* carrier bag.

It was a fifteen-minute walk to Davie and Terasa's. On the way they stopped to buy cigarettes at the local mini-market. As they left the store an estate car tooted its horn and the passenger leaned out and shouted 'Away The Mental!' The recognition made The Kid blush a bit, although he had no idea who it was.

An old man who looked about eighty passed them on the street and said 'Hello, there' to Mental. 'That guy's eighty-six,' said Mental, hand atop his mouth. 'He's Celtic daft. He only stopped going on the bus last season.'

They, or rather Mental, talked about football. Archie said Aberdeen would win the league easily and Mental was off. He seemed more obsessed with the hip tradition of Celtic than by the loathsomeness of Glasgow Rangers. Celtic's youth policy, good-looking supporters, the hip pop stars all supported Celtic. 'As I always say, name me one good-looking guy that's ever played for Rangers. You can't, it's impossible.' The language of cliché abounded as Mental talked: 'Big Roy's a great motivator ... obviously ... at the end of the day ... 110 per cent effort;' during the fifteen-minute walk, Archie guessed that The Kid said eight 'obviouslys' and twenty 'we's' — the rebel 'we', Celtic and their supporters.

Six

Terasa opened the door of number 45 Turnberry Gardens after Mental knocked. She wore bleached Levi's slit at both knees and an XL white T-shirt. Her hair was starting to grow out of the wet-look perm she'd had done a while back. She was twenty-two. The previous summer she and Davie split up for two months after an argument about going on holiday. They had been going out for seven years. During the split, Terasa went out with Mental a couple of times for someone to talk to. Then, one night, Mental turned up with a bottle of wine and dirty intentions. Terasa told him to fuck off. Archie was unsure what had happened and how much Davie knew. 'Nothing happened,' was all The Kid would say. It always seemed strange to Archie that two people could live together and keep secrets from each other and yet he knew Davie and Terasa did: that bloke Terasa went out with during the split, that girl Davie was with a couple of New Years ago and the lies Davie told about money. There was also the question of Mental's attitude to Terasa. When Davie first started going out with her, Mental was manifestly in awe. He used to grab her all the time and have kid-on fights. Davie said that he and Terasa had a few good laughs at Mental's expense.

But Archie suspected they had a few good arguments as well.

'We have come to sing you songs and tell you jokes,' announced Mental.

'Come in, both of you.'

In the living-room, Big Davie was asleep in a big comfy chair, his feet supported by the coffee table. Horace the kitten purred contentedly on his lap.

'You've knackered the Hun,' said Mental to Terasa. Terasa scorned him. Dave lay happily in the land of Z.

The room smelled of chicken curry. Vestas were the staple diet. Archie sat on the settee and lit a cigarette hoping to stir Davie accidentally-on-purpose. He failed. Mental walked over to the storage heater and sat on it.

'Hey you. We've got chairs,' said Terasa. 'Sit beside Archie.'

'I'm not sitting beside him,' retorted Mental. 'He's got dirty boots on.'

Archie looked shamefaced at his boots. They were caked in mud. Guilty bits of hardened mud formed a trail from the door to the settee. Terasa shook her head and said, 'Have you ever brushed those boots?'

Archie could say nothing.

'You could make yourself a lot more respectable, you know that?' continued Terasa. Archie blushed phone-box red. He felt like a footballer trying to be articulate, searching for the appropriate cliché. The only word that entered his head was 'obviously'. 'Mental might go around wearing the recently departed's old suits,' added Terasa, 'but at least he makes an effort.' Archie and Mental looked at each other and faked crying.

'Oh, shut up, the pair of you and help me finish this bottle of wine.'

As they drank the wine, Big Davie slept on. Archie and Mental were amused but Terasa looked anxious. Every day when he came home, he took a nap — and the forty winks became four hundred.

'He didn't get any sleep last night, remember,' said Mental.

'He slept for a couple of hours before he left,' said Terasa.

'When people have problems they can't sleep,' offered Archie.

'I don't think he sleeps at night.' Terasa stared at Mental and Archie looking helpless. Terasa was confiding and Archie felt like shit; stupid, selfish and useless. This wasn't a car that needed a push.

'He's okay,' assured Mental. 'He hates his work. He worries about you, you know. He doesn't think he's good enough for you.'

'He's stopped smoking,' added Terasa. 'I came home and he told me he'd rather have a night out than to keep smoking.' Davie had smoked since he was fifteen. Many would have thought it more likely for Ian Paisley to record a cover version of *The Wild Rover*.

'Can I go over and kiss him?' said Mental. 'For a laugh, like.'

'No,' said Terasa.

'You going out tonight?' asked Archie.

'Kate Dunlop's having her show of presents. I said I'd pop round about nine.' Terasa looked at the clock.

The kitten flew off Davie's stomach as if anticipating some disturbance.

'Ahhhhhhhhhhhhhhhhhhhhhh. When did you lot arrive?' yawned Davie.

'Couple of hours ago,' lied Mental. 'You've got some gut, ya fat bastard.'

'Must've dozed off. Your boots are in some fucking state, Archie.' They all laughed and everything seemed okay.

'I need the bathroom,' said Mental.

'Just a minute,' said Terasa.

'You better get your underwear out of there before he gets his nose stuck in.' Davie laughed at his joke and made a rude gesture.

Archie played with Horace the kitten, amused by its frailty. 'How would you like to meet my pal Dostoyevsky?' Archie asked the kitten. The big word terrified Horace. It was the biggest he'd ever heard. The Dobermann would probably have induced heart failure.

'Okay. The throne awaits you.' Terasa wasn't bothered about the underwear. A wee jobby had refused the flush earlier and she was pushing it round the S-bend with

43

the aid of some toilet paper. She removed the underwear, anyway.

Davie shook the bottle of wine. Empty. Terasa went into the kitchen and brought a cloth back to wipe the table where she had spilt some wine. She turned the cloth over and polished the table. Mental returned.

'Tell them about Carol,' said Terasa. Carol was Davie's younger sister.

'What's this? What's this?' Mental anticipated gossip.

'She's moving in with a guy called Liam!'

'Brilliant. You're joking,' cried Mental. 'Your dad'll be going spare. Magic.'

'"Furtive," he says.' Terasa adopted a gruff man's voice. '"It's all furtive."'

'That's the thing,' said Davie. 'It's been on the cards for about three months. Even *we* didn't know about it.'

'"Furtive. It's all furtive." I hope they get married in a chapel.'

'What time's the fight on?' said Davie, studying the TV page.

'Eight o'clock. ITV. After *Coronation Street*,' said Archie, struck by the resemblance of Davie to his father in asking the question.

'Your dad's a right Orange bastard, eh?' said Mental still amused by the story of Carol and Liam. 'He's really ugly as well. Mind that guy mistook him for Bobby Shearer.' Mental roared with laughter.

'That was the proudest day of my dad's life.' Davie laughed but he didn't like Mental slagging his dad. It hurt a bit.

Terasa switched on the TV and picked up the remote control. *Coronation Street*. A collection of weel kent faces appeared on the screen, like old neighbours. Archie tried to pick up the story.

Before Big Davie started work, Mental and Archie were round at the house most days. They lay about watching daytime television, drinking tea and listening to records. Maybe go down the town, place a bet, get some messages. Now, Mental and Archie only came round at night and occasionally on Sunday afternoons. Terasa never went out of her way to make them feel uncomfortable, it just wasn't convenient. Archie and Mental went to Richard's when they wanted to slob out.

Coronation Street stopped for a commercial break.

'When are you going to decorate this place then?' Archie asked Terasa.

'Welllllllllll, it's funny you should say that because we'd like you two to strip the walls next Tuesday. We're both off on Wednesday afternoon so we thought the four of us could get the job done Wednesday afternoon and night. That paper'll be difficult to come off. There's five layers.' Terasa bit her lower lip.

'I sign on next Tuesday,' said Mental, trying to exert some influence.

'Not all day you don't,' pointed out Terasa. 'I want my good paper — have you seen it? — on that wall . . .'

'And the cheap shit everywhere else,' completed Mental.

'I just want you two for the mundane work: scraping, painting and tidying up. Understand? I don't want you doing anything that requires skill. Okay?'

'We understand,' said The Kid. 'We're fucking useless. Don't trust us with anything more than a scraper or a paintbrush.'

'As long as you understand that,' said Terasa, not joking.

Archie and Mental would each get a tenner for their work, and Terasa would make them earn it. She could have let Davie do it all but his mind seemed to be on other things. They had lived in the house for three months. It was her idea to get a place of their own. The mortgage took up most of her wage. Her father was a wealthy man who would provide money if she needed it. She may have been a rebel who went against her parents' wishes, but had the circumstances arisen she would not think twice about asking for money. Since the age of sixteen, she had worked for a firm of accountants and took night classes to improve her education. Davie was not as well organised. No qualifications, no trade. A bakery where he had happily worked for a couple of years made him redundant and closed down shortly afterwards. They lived in what Kelly called 'Spam Valley'; where people were so tied to their mortgages they never went out, had holidays or ate decent meals.

Coronation Street finished with Eric Spears' haunting lament: Tra-la-dee-da-dee-da.

Mental picked up the remote control (RC he called it) and flicked through the channels. 'When you getting married?' he asked.

'Whenever she wants,' said Davie showing his palms.

'Ian Paisley's fully booked up just now. It'll be a while yet,' teased Terasa.

'You should convert to Catholicism. Graham Greene did. It's a lot more spiritual. Fuck the dogma, like.' Mental could praise and condemn Catholicism all night.

They settled to watch the boxing. Mental lit a cigarette, Archie extinguished his. Davie sniffed the air and said, 'That's five hours I've gone without one.'

'I'm going to stop soon,' said Mental. 'My financial situation is getting dire. Fancy popping round to Richard's to smoke some shit later?'

'Sure.'

'Try and scrounge a joint's worth off him,' said Terasa. She sat on her ankles pointing her exposed knees.

Davie picked up the remote control and adjusted the volume clumsily. He settled back into his chair, arms folded and legs crossed at the ankles. Horace, the kitten, saw a spider running towards the storage heater and followed at speed. The spider got behind the storage heater and Horace commenced a stakeout.

Watching the boxing the second time round, Archie bit his fingernails where previously he had bitten his knuckles. The buzzwords of the liberals meant nothing: barbaric, brain scan/damage. Marvin Hagler was no Bertrand Russell but he was as articulate as any footballer. The latter were always showered and dressed before being interviewed by their commentator friends. The interviews were recorded and everybody was trotting out their clichés. When a boxer wins a gruelling battle he has to overcome exhaustion and euphoria. 'I'M THE FUCKING WORLD CHAMPION!'

After the fight, Jim Watt grudgingly praised Hagler but reserved most of his comment for saying that Hearns fought the wrong fight — you don't mix it with Hagler. On the commentary, the brilliant welterweight champion Don Currie said much the same thing.

'Do you think Currie could take Hagler?' asked Davie. Davie didn't share Archie's knowledge of or passion for boxing. In truth, Davie didn't have much time for anything. He'd have difficulty in selecting a specialist subject for *Mastermind*. Maybe football.

'By the time Currie's established himself at middleweight, Hagler'll have retired,' said Archie. 'Hagler should be more worried about John Mugabe and Herol Graham.'

'Herol Graham could take Hagler,' declared Mental. 'He's got that cockiness about him, you know what I mean? That poofy voice and everything.'

'Well,' said Terasa, 'I'd better get ready if I'm going.' She disappeared upstairs.

'Do you just want to go over to Richard's just now then?' said The Kid. 'He's taping the programme for you anyway.'

'I suppose so,' said Archie. 'My dad's taping it too.'

'My better half doesn't like you two being in here when she's out, anyway.' Davie rubbed his nose and made a face.

'I resent that,' said The Kid. 'I could understand that tramp,' Mental indicated Archie, 'being mistaken for a carrier of pestilence but I . . .'

'"*Pestilence*"?' repeated Archie. 'Where did that come from?'

'He must have heard it on the bus,' said Davie. 'Sounds like something you'd hear in a rebel song. "Oh the pestilence is spreading over Ire-land brought and left to rot by the English-man".'

'I don't know,' said Mental agitated. 'I just . . . I must've picked it up somewhere, obviously, I wouldn't have said the thing otherwise, would I?'

'Rebel song,' said Davie.

Mental was getting wound up. That little vein was sticking out on his forehead. 'Yeah, sure, Davie. Exactly right. One of The Wolftones' classics. "Never heard of Sean O'Casey, George Bernard Shaw, Samuel Beckett, Eugene O'Neill, Edna O'Brien and Laurence Sterne",' sang Mental quoting Dexy's Midnight Runners' classic 'Dance Stance/Burn it Down'.

47

'George Bernard Shaw supported Hitler during World War Two,' said Davie. 'What's so good about him?'

'Oh, he was senile then,' dismissed Mental. 'For a small nation, Ireland has produced an incredible number of great writers, and great footballers. I'd like to see your Scotland with Liam Brady and Kevin Sheedy and Mark Lawrenson. It's amazing they've got such a crap team.' Mental shook his head in bafflement.

Since the Scottish support had started jeering black players, Archie had lost all interest in the Scottish national team. He preferred to see them get beat. Mental had always supported Eire. Davie still went to all Scotland's matches and was angry and upset when they got beat.

'How well are your Glasgow Rangers doing anyway?' teased Mental.

'We're just going through one of our crises, that's all.'

Terasa re-entered. She was wearing a mushroom-coloured corduroy skirt suit with a V-neck cream-coloured jumper and a thin gold chain around her neck. She looked gorgeous.

'Ta-ra,' she said. There were whistles and claps of approval.

'You look a bit bare around the neck,' said Davie. He looked at her as if he just realised how much he loved her.

'I'll be all right,' said Terasa, smiling.

'You're too good for that Hun,' said Mental. 'And with a name like Terasa, too. Dearie dear.'

'There's no Irish or Catholic in me, I'm afraid.'

'I love that name. Te-ray-za. Wonderful.' Mental looked overwhelmed.

'Terasa's a good name,' said Archie, 'but Marvin's better.' They all laughed.

'I prefer Marvin Gaye,' said Terasa. She sang *Let's Get It On* while picking up a set of keys and putting them in a green clutch bag.

'You taking the van?' asked The Kid. 'You going to drop us off?'

'No. It's out of my way.'

'Oh, come on. Somebody might attack us.' It was the only argument he could think of.

'Well, I'm going,' said Terasa and went over to Davie. 'Kiss before I go.' They kissed.

'What about me?' enquired The Kid.

'What indeed,' said Terasa enigmatically. 'I'll see you later. Cheerio, Horace.' Horace continued his vigil at the storage heater without moving an eyelid. Terasa left and the motor could be heard turning. It started first time.

She never said cheerio to me, noticed Archie, truly upset. What a bastard!

'She's a bit worried about you, you know,' said Mental to Davie.

'I know. I know. I don't need you to tell me that. It's just the work gets me down. There's a new guy starting tomorrow. Syme thinks he's God. Some English guy. He's got him on our wagon.'

'Is that the guy called Tesco?' asked Archie. Davie nodded.

'We seen him earlier,' said The Kid. 'The ugliest guy I ever seen in my life.'

'Does Syme say anything about Terasa?' asked Archie, tentatively.

'NO!' Davie stared Archie in the face. 'I AM NOT THAT SOFT.'

On the television screen Marvin Hagler was saying that Tommy Hearns had been getting a bit cocky and needed to be taught a lesson.

'Let's pass the tu-sheng-peng,' Mental announced. '"Tu-sheng-peng make I count from one to ten",' sang Mental in the worst Jamaican accent this side of Sting.

'Yeah, let's go.' Davie put on his trainers, jerkin and bunnet. He switched off the TV and pulled out the plug.

'Cheerio, Horace,' said Archie.

As Davie turned out the light, the spider emerged, only to discover the peculiar qualities of cats' eyes.

49

Seven

'YEAHHHHHHHHHHHHHH!!!!!'

'What the fuck was that?' shrieked Mental.

'Those bastards leaning out that car,' said Davie. 'I thought it was the brakes. They were screaming their fucking heads off.'

Motorists took special routes in order to build up speed and utilise power. Taunting pedestrians was an option, a pleasant option.

Archie tried to imagine the people who lived in the flats. Were they watching TV? How often did they get phone calls? Did they take drugs? Were they happy? It was impossible ... like trying to imagine yourself with a different face, or being brought up in Canada or Calcutta.

'Garbage. Davie Provan is miles better than Davie Cooper.' The Kid was talking football. 'Provan's got pace and he can cross a ball. Cooper's a great dribbler, granted, but he's that slow he never gets anywhere. He scores the odd free kick against the Mickey Mouse teams and the Hun press say he's great. Did you hear the one about Davie McPherson using the Maradona videos for his training?' Mental was desperate to tell the joke for the hundredth time.

'And he goes like this,' said Davie mocking Mental's over-enthusiastic delivery of the punchline by kneeling and crossing himself.

'What do you call an Irishman with ten pricks?' asked Archie.

'Ancient. Ancient,' said Mental. 'And not funny.'

'Those jokes have been handed down through generations,' said Davie. 'There are young lads who think they are brand new. It's like I used to think Wee Stevie invented the word "fuck". Straight up. He said it all the time — still does — like it was his word. He said it in front of teachers, in front of his ma, everybody. I thought he invented it. I mind when I went to see my first X-certificate I was astonished to hear all these Americans saying Wee Stevie's word. 'Member that time . . .'

Archie remembered: Wee Stevie avoiding the belt from tin-dick Frazer, after drinking sodium hydroxide; Wee Stevie inventing zubb-dubbs (heartily chewed pieces of paper) and throwing them at blackboards and girls; Wee Stevie's encyclopaedia of sick jokes and the problems of Wee Stevie never wearing underwear. Davie had a million stories about Wee Stevie and about school. If Mental showed his age by resorting to cliché, then Davie showed his by romanticising the past. Wee Stevie was funny but he was also devious and callous. He had let a lot of people down over the years. He had plans and ambitions which would never come to fruition, yet he talked about them earnestly and frequently. Richard had told him, 'Your bullshit's like your BO; it doesn't seem to bother you but it gets up other people's noses.' Stevie had no qualms about turning up at people's doorsteps at any time. He would stay for half an hour, saying little, but thankful for the company. Women adored him.

Davie had a great memory for detail. He mentioned the name Rachael Morrison and Archie recalled a fat girl with long black hair who always wore a red jumper. Davie could reel off everyone he had ever been at school with: what teachers, what years, what happened. It was as easy as recalling the nine times table — maybe even easier. Davie was even better at telling stories after he'd had a drink. Trouble was they were always the same stories and they dated from way back. Recent history was the specialist subject of The Mental Kid. Information passed through his household with a greater turnover than the BBC World Service newsdesk.

They arrived at Richard's block of flats and Mental rushed to play *A Soldier's Song* on the entryphone buzzer.

'Yeah.'

'Let us in. It's freezing out here.'

'All right. Davie and Archie can come up, but the Leon Brittan lookalike can fuck off.'

Mental's flabber was gasted. 'Leon Brittan,' he said. 'Leon Brittan!' He looked as if someone had brought him shit in a restaurant. It was a ridiculous comparison, reasoned Mental. Obviously it was a joke. It was like saying the Pope looked like, eh . . . Charles Manson. ALTERNATIVE COMEDY!!! That was it.

As they ascended to the top (fourth) floor, the gentle thud of a reggae beat grew louder. Davie let himself in and Archie and Mental followed.

'Come in,' said Richard. 'I'm just trying to keep Dostoyevsky calm.'

Dostoyevsky was far from calm. He could smell all manner of exotica: Jinky, Horace, stewed steak, chicken curry.

'I hate alternative comedy,' said The Kid to the bafflement of all. 'All these middle-class creeps faking middle-class accents. What's the point? Put on your Richard Pryor video.'

'No. Not tonight. Some other time.'

The living-room was arranged to accommodate Dostoyevsky: everything was back against the walls leaving a big space in the centre for him to stretch out. Against one wall was a hi-fi, eleven hundred LPs and three thousand singles. Richard kept all his records catalogued in his computer. He kept charts like most popular LP artist (Elvis Costello), most popular singles artist (James Brown), most popular cover version (*For Your Precious Love*). The record collection was insured but Richard would never say how much for. Guesstimates, though, were about ten thousand pounds.

A bookcase and a couple of easy chairs were against the opposite wall. The bookcase contained mostly music encyclopaedias and biographies, with a smattering of paper-backs, and twenty self-compiled music videos. Elsewhere there was a sideboard, a settee and a dining-room table. The latter was covered with music papers, magazines, mail order lists and library books. The walls were covered in posters, pictures and postcards: Captain Beefheart, *Erazerhead*, Lee Perry, *The Blues Brothers*, The Temptations, Winston Rodney, Jim Morrison, The Clash and many more.

'I'm going to let him go,' said Richard. Archie had removed his jacket and was stretching his fingers. He picked up a long, yellow tube and held it in front of him, swaying it from side to side. Dostoyevsky followed the motion with his head, Richard let him go. Dostoyevsky moved calmly across the room. Archie checked his grip. Dostoyevsky grabbed the other end with his mouth and pulled like hell.

'Come on, Dostoyevsky,' cried The Kid. 'Beat the scruff.'

'He's winning. He's winning,' said Davie.

'Is he fuck,' said Archie. Dostoyevsky growled and shook his head vigorously. Archie adjusted his grip. His knuckles were white.

Suddenly, the tube snapped and Dostoyevsky flew back-wards towards the bookcase. A small piece of yellow plastic tube in his mouth.

'Tough shit, Dostoyevsky. You got beat,' said Mental.

Dostoyevsky picked up the rest of the tube and offered Archie an end. His eyes said 'Round Two'.

'No, that's enough for tonight, Dostoyevsky.' Archie pat-ted the dog on the head.

Dostoyevsky offered the tube to Davie: 'I've got a bad back.' To Mental: 'I'm just a wimp. You'd beat me no problem.'

Dostoyevsky did his Cocker Spaniel impression complete with whine. It was pathetic.

'How about a low five?' asked Archie. Dostoyevsky drop-ped the tube and offered a paw.

'Right, it's time for your bed, dog.' Richard headed towards the door. Dostoyevsky followed reluctantly. A pissed-off pinscher.

Davie walked over to the sideboard and picked up a small plastic bag and a packet of cigarette papers. Mental handed him an LP cover (The Royal Rasses' *Humanity* which Richard had been playing upon their arrival) and his packet of Marlboro. 'Use these,' he said.

'The master craftsman at work,' said Richard. Davie was the only one present who could roll a good smoke. Mental was enthusiastically hopeless while Archie and Richard were just ordinary hopeless.

'Davie's stopped smoking,' said Mental.

'Good man,' said Richard. 'When did you stop?'

'This afternoon. But that's me for good. I'm looking forward to this, though.'

'Take some home for Terasa,' said Richard.

'Right, thanks.' Davie offered no money because Richard would have refused.

'Put on *Funhouse*,' said Mental as *Humanity* finished. 'Iggy is God.' Richard went over to the hi-fi.

He played the record at a respectable volume considering the time of night. Iggy grunted a few times before commencing *Down in the Street*: 'Yeah, deep in the night/I'm lost in love,' he sang. The Rolling Stones' *Beggar's Banquet*'s American cousin, *Funhouse* sounded just as it ought to: raw, dirty, nihilistic. 'I stick it deep inside when I'm *loose*.' Awesome. 'She gotta TV Eye on me/she gotta a TV Eye.' Sometimes it was difficult to appreciate familiar records in company but not tonight. When the long and mellow *Dirt* ('Do you feel it when you touch me?') was under way, Mental spoke.

'That shit wasn't up to much. Did you say you got it off Wee Stevie?'

'Yeah. I don't know where he gets it. His deals are crap.'

'It's a bit boring, that track,' said Mental. 'Turn it over and play *1970* and *Funhouse*.'

'No. What do you want to hear, Archie?'

'Miles Davis, *Blue in Green*.' Archie was becoming obsessed with Miles Davis and he was loving it.

'That's really beautiful,' said Davie as Miles played. 'Makes you wish you could play an instrument.' Davie had nowhere the same number of records as Archie, Mental or Richard, but he always showed his appreciation of things he liked.

Mental spoke as the track finished. 'Better than all that fusion shit he did. Those massive drumkits, massive keyboards and John McLaughlin. Dearie dear.'

'Right, Davie, your choice,' said Richard.

'I've no idea. Just you pick.'

'Put on *Pride*,' said Mental.

'Cliché,' said Richard. 'Typical Celtic supporter's choice. You're supposed to choose something different when you come up here, you know.' Richard was teasing, he loved the record too. He found the single and put it on.

'It's incredible the number of major singers that are Catholics,' said The Kid. 'Especially when you consider what a Hun country this is: you've got Elvis, Lydon, Steven, *Patrick* Morrissey, Patrick MacAloon, Kevin Rowland, Bono . . .'

'Bono's Irish,' said Richard.

'You know what I mean!' said The Kid. He looked as if someone had just produced a video of him singing *Land of Ho-o-ope and Glo-o-ory.*

'So you think . . .' started Davie.

'Okay. Okay. I was wrong. End of conversation.'

'They took your life/But they could not take your Pride,' sang Bono on the tribute to Dr Martin Luther King. The record finished.

'Peel'll be on,' said Archie.

Richard flicked some switches and The Smiths came booming out the speakers just to remind everyone who the greatest group in the history of the universe was. The track, *Nowhere Fast.*

'*Meat is Murder*, an LP of the Year?' asked John Peel.

'There are more important things in the world to get worked up about than carnivores,' said Davie, a Smiths hater. 'They still eat eggs and food cooked in animal fat, *and* they wear leather shoes.'

'Peel's a veggie, eh?' said The Kid.

'Yeah,' said Richard. 'Would you go out and kill an animal for food?'

'People are paid to do it. It's their job,' said Davie. 'I bet you wouldn't take out your own appendix. Anyway, Hitler was a veggie and I didn't like him.'

'Medical reasons,' said Richard.

Through the wall, a Dobermann dreamed of sausages.

'I just can't relate meat to a living thing,' said Mental. 'Last Sunday, my mum and dad went through to see my granny in Greenock. So me and Kelly decided to make an omelette for the tea. So I started grating this lump of chopped ham and pork for the filling. Grating it! The only reason it bothered me was because it didn't bother me.'

Richard saw a chicken's face being pushed against a grater; bloody and screaming. He said, 'When you look out of a train or whatever and you see sheep and cattle, don't you think about what's going to happen to them? They don't have a clue what's going to happen to them. I hate the politics of food: the way the Third World produces grain as a cash crop for export to America so they can feed their fat docile cattle, so they can make hamburgers to make fat bastards — nothing personal, Davie — while the peoples of the Third World starve.'

'It's too much hassle,' said Mental.

'Too much hassle,' repeated Richard. 'I suppose it was too much hassle to support the miners, the ANC, the IRA.' Richard had collected for the miners and got kicked by a pensioner on the day the taxi driver was killed.

'I supported the miners' cause,' said The Kid, 'but they were arseholes. They were thick and they were proud of being thick. Your average miner couldn't articulate. Okay, maybe they would have come across better in a suit, in a studio in a relaxed atmosphere, whathaveyou.' Mental anticipated Richard's 'media bias' argument. 'But I don't really think so. They were like Scotland supporters. They'll vote Labour until they die but they'll go to Hampden and shout "Sambo, Sambo". How many striking miners said "Fuck off" when they were offered a job in South Africa, eh? The papers were full of those adverts. And that is the lowest of the low, going there. Anybody that goes there deserves all they're going to get. Of course I support the ANC. If I had a bomb I'd give it to them and I wouldn't bother if they used it on a whites-only maternity ward. Fuck all this talk of tragedy: bomb the bastards, hack them to death, stone them to death. You know who McGahey reminded me of? He was like a South

African politician; so smug, so above the law, so above the media. And as for the IRA; remember you are talking to the guy that did cartwheels on the day of the Brighton bombing.'

'He 'phoned me up,' said Archie, 'screaming "She's been bombed! She's been bombed!"'

'They said on the telly the entire nation was horrified,' continued The Kid. 'Fucking garbage. Old Chrissie Davis was dancing down the street.'

John Peel rambled on about receiving a letter from Caldercruix — 'I think that's how you pronounce it' — requesting information about old session tapes. 'It's a crying shame,' said the nation's collective Uncle John, 'that more of our stuff isn't more readily available.' Twenty years spent trying to lose a hideous upper-class accent had paid off for John, and he sounded lovely. You have to work at these things.

Richard said, 'Fancy a game of golf some time, Davie?'

'I hate golf,' said Mental to the surprise of no one save a few undiscovered tribes in the Amazon basin. 'It spoils a good walk.'

'Iggy plays golf,' said Archie. 'Gotta lust for golf.'

'I'll only believe Iggy plays golf when I see him on telly with Jimmy Tarbuck and Bruce Forsyth and all those fascists. I think you're all having me on.' Mental couldn't handle Iggy playing golf. It was like Pat Nevin playing for Chelsea.

'I don't know about getting the cash . . .' started Davie.

'Oh, stop moaning about money,' said Mental. 'I'll give you my UB40. Nobody'll arrest you.'

'Don't know about that,' said Richard. 'Impersonating an obnoxious Catholic is a serious offence. And how about starting up the football again?'

'Yeah,' said Mental. 'I'm into that.'

'Well, from a week on Friday, we're off every Friday. And we finish at two on Tuesdays,' said Davie.

'So I'll book up the football for a week on Friday. How about the golf?'

'How about a week on Tuesday, after work?' Davie sounded well cheered now.

'Fine by me, I'll see you before then to finalise it.' Richard always felt Davie was left out of the conversations. His concerns were always more practical than spiritual, more local than global. 'Any date fixed for the wedding?'

Mental saved Davie the trouble of having to answer: 'Reading between the lines I think it's going to be soon.'

'First it's when you going to get engaged? Then when you going to get married? When you going to start a family? I do think about these things. I think about them all the time. It's just that sometimes I think . . . I don't know. We make really good friends and . . . I don't see us like the couples you see on quiz shows.'

'OH, FOR FUCK'S SAKE,' cried Mental. '*They* are the scum of the earth! You're way above them. All those George Benson fans. Dearie dear.'

'These people are so plastic,' said Richard. 'TV homogenises everything. They have to look the same. They have to talk the same. They're only good at quiz programmes because they watch them all the time. It's their training. My mum's pretty thick but she can answer a fair proportion of the questions on *Blockbusters*. She's been training for years.'

'You can always spot the Orangemen on game shows,' said Mental. 'They've always got on long sleeves to hide their tattoos.' Everybody laughed. 'It's true. Honest.'

'My mum and dad watch all the quiz shows,' said Archie. 'They're good at them.'

'The best television programme ever was *Freewheelers*,' said Mental.

'You always say that,' said Davie, 'but nobody can remember a programme of that name. I think you're bullshitting.'

'I'm not. I'm not. It was on a Tuesday. Ten to five. It had these kids saving the world. It was a serial. I always wanted to grow up quickly so as I could be the same age as the kids in the programme. I also liked the first series of *Happy Days* and *Rich Man, Poor Man*.'

'I still say the best TV programme ever was the very first series of *Scooby Doo*,' asserted Archie.

'Hear, hear,' said Davie. 'Mind we got our picture in the *Daily Record* complaining to the BBC about the second series.'

'The second series was garbage,' explained Archie, 'and we wrote to the BBC with a massive petition saying that they should repeat the first series instead of showing the crappy new stuff. And we ended up with our picture in the paper.'

'This guy here,' Davie indicated Archie, 'was really worked up about it. Everybody else treated it as a half-joke, you know. But Archie, he was howling.'

'Well,' blushed Archie, 'the second series was crap.'

'That's like when we used to have mass battles at school,' said Richard, 'I was the one that was really into it. I would get really worked up. Everybody else would just be pushing each other and trading insults. Me, though, I would be getting really stuck in. Everybody would gather round to watch me beating shit out of some poor guy. They wondered what he'd done to upset me, and I would say, "I thought we were supposed to be fighting them." It was really weird.'

'Mind that time we went down Tay Street?' said Mental to Davie and Archie. 'Just before they pulled the buildings down?'

'That was a great day, that,' said Davie. Archie smiled in agreement.

Mental stared Richard in the eye. 'All the houses were empty, they were just waiting to be flattened, so we went down there one afternoon and we smashed everything: every window, every door, *everything*. We stayed the whole afternoon. It was great. We threw stones, rocks, bricks, anything. Inside as well: we tore apart the banisters, tore off the doors, smashed the cupboards, the lot. Nobody bothered us. I'm telling you it was real Millwall stuff.'

'You really enjoyed that day,' said Davie.

'I know. I know. That's what I recall the most vividly; being happy.'

'Anyway, I better get going,' said Davie. 'Thanks for the smoke and the blether. Terasa wants to go out for a drink tomorrow. Will we see you down the pub?'

'I wouldn't mind going out tomorrow,' said Richard. 'I want to see Bob about some records.' Bob Johnson was the DJ at their pub.

'Got to rush back to the little woman, eh?' teased Mental.

'I'd rather have a stable monogamous relationship than your six-in-a-bed-and-one-of-them's-called-Rover idea of a good time.'

'I'm not like that. Everything gets exaggerated because it's me,' Mental was blushing with anger. I blush therefore I am.

'Your baldness isn't getting any better, Davie,' said Richard.

'Just a high hairline, that's all,' lied Davie.

'Funny place to have a hairline,' said The Kid. 'On the top of your head.'

'I don't know what Richard's acting so superior about, he was the guy that liked *Mr Blue Sky*.' Davie swung a parting shot.

'Oh no, here we go.' Richard buried his head in his lap. 'This is not true. This is just not true.'

'It is,' charged Mental. 'My big sister says that when you used to take her down the *Royal*, you always played that on the jukebox.'

'She just says that to hurt me. It was the exact opposite. I hated that record.' Richard was resigned. He had dumped Mental's big sister and she told a hurtful, spiteful lie about him.

'And,' said Mental adopting the tone of an investigative journalist, 'what was the first record that you ever bought? I mean what was the musical milestone that so fuelled your enthusiasm that you procured the best personal record collection this side of John Peel?'

'You know,' said Richard. He stood up, hands on hips.

'I put it to you that the first record you ever bought was that classic of contemporary beat, that protest song's protest song *Chirpy Chirpy Cheep Cheep*. What do you have to say to this then?' Everybody laughed including Richard. When Mental was trying to be funny people generally laughed at him not with him, so precise and devoid of irony was his mode of delivery.

'I don't believe that the first three singles you bought were the first three Roxy singles.' Richard shook his head. 'No fucking way.'

'They were. The second and third were bought on the day of release. Swear to God.' Mental smiled with pride. Archie's first record was *Twenty Fantastic Hits Volume II* (bought mainly for *Jean Genie* and *Blockbuster*), and Davie's was *Moon River* by Greyhound. 'I've always had great taste,' continued Mental. 'I might not have the same range of appreciation as you, but my taste is immaculate.'

'I didn't like *Mr Blue Sky*. Honest.' This point was really important to Richard.

'I'll have to run,' said Davie. 'Cheerio, lads.'

'See you,' said Richard. 'I'll get in touch about the golf and the football.'

'Are your clubs at your ma's?' asked Davie.

'No, they're in Dostoyevsky's room. Were you wanting to see them?'

'No. No. It's okay. See you.' Davie left. Let sleeping dogs lie . . . lest they might kill you.

Eight

At school Richard had been the boy most likely. He won a debating competition and collected A-grade Highers with ease. When punk came along in '76/'77 Richard embraced it. Only two copies of *Anarchy in the UK* reached town: Richard got one and Senga Somerville the other. At youth clubs and school discos, Richard acted as DJ playing Shirley and Co's *Shame Shame Shame* while his friends were listening to *Tales from Topographic Oceans*. Richard was first to wear an anti-Nazi League badge. Students who took part in the sit-ins to protest against the Biafran war would later admit to taking part 'just for fun': punk seemed different. Those who marched against the loathsome National Front in Lewisham projected an intensity of feeling. It was unfortunate that not all such demonstrations were as well motivated and executed. Too many causes were led by the ill-informed and supported by the ignorant. Mental said that pickets and demonstrators aspired to strength through exploitation and intimidation. It wasn't honest like arguing and fighting.

Richard read avidly the music press of the late seventies: Julie Burchill, Tony Parsons, Jane Suck, Jonh Ingham, Jon Savage and the old guard: Charles Shaar Murray, Giovanni

Dadomo and Nick Kent. Julie continued to write, adopting an extreme position then justifying it. She slagged off Catholics, worshipped Russia and supported Maggie in the Falklands. (Richard wrote into *The Face* saying that although Julie was right to support the fight against a Fascist junta, the British public would always be more motivated by the xenophobic side of the conflict.) Jon Savage became an art groupie. Tony Parsons wrote three bile-filled novels that never fully showed his talent. (His review of the first Clash LP was stuck on Richard's wall. Now *that* was writing.) Jane Suck became Jane Solanas, superdyke. Nick Kent's signature appeared at the end of a few articles but they didn't seem very enthusiastic. He loved The Smiths, though. As for the others Richard didn't know where they were. He presumed they'd given up and gone fat. One of Richard's deepest regrets was that he hadn't kept a chart of his most played records. He knew, though, that Parsons' and Burchill's *The Boy Looked at Johnny* was the book he had read most. While punk in the south attracted the arse-end of the media (high and low-brow), the provinces adopted the 'No Fun', 'No Feelings', 'No Future' triumvirate as dogma and it stuck like glue. Pun intended. The legacy of Sid Vicious meant spiky tops, leather jackets, The UK Subs, Oi and circles with A in the middle. Richard, though, continued to wear his anti-Nazi League badge through Tom Robinson, The Gang of Four, *Cut, London Calling,* Paul Morley and Dave McCullough.

Richard thought he'd be intimidated at university. He expected to meet people who knew everything about Dylan, Kafka and Scorsese. He was wrong, of course. The spirit of the Biafra sit-ins reigned. Like the hippies who had never heard of Muddy Waters and the punks who never bought any reggae, the students never did more than they had to. Richard left his degree course in English at the end of the third year. 'I wanted to be trained in logic,' he told Archie. 'I wanted to be educated to the extent whereby I no longer made stupid mistakes about things. I wanted common sense. One of my teachers at school said that he had been trained in logic at university. He was completely cool. He could see through lies like that. Everything was rational for him.

I wanted something like that to take away all the hassles and pressures.'

When Susan Jones dumped him on a wet Tuesday evening in 1984, she ended a three-year friendship and eighteen months of living together. 'What *are* you talking about?' she would say, oblivious to his problems and paranoias. He'd spent so long bettering himself to avoid feeling inferior he became frightening and intimidating. He was always right in every argument. Mental hated Susan Jones with a fervour more commonly reserved for Glasgow Rangers and Midge Ure's singing. He said she was thick and that Richard was well rid of her. Richard, though, suffered from a dull ache behind the ears; one minute his head would feel as if it was filled with lead and the next filled with helium. At nights he would turn the pillows until they were boiling, vainly trying to get some sleep. The doctor said it was anxiety and told him to sleep regular hours; asleep no later than twelve. Richard still went nights without sleep and would go for days without talking to anyone. Susan wrote and said she thought of him. Richard tore the letters to bits. For a while he got an erection while he was angry. He couldn't understand why. He didn't feel in the slightest bit sexual and he would never hurt anyone. When Susan lived with him they contributed to a late-night phone-in programme called *Transistor Boogie*. They phoned up every week. The DJ always went on about what a lovely couple they were. The regular contributors still mentioned them in their dedications.

Richard analysed all his faults and came up with some horrible conclusions. He looked forward to a time when he would stop feeling sorry for himself. When he would be fat, he presumed. He wrote to Susan saying that he missed her as a friend. She wrote back saying that she was going out with a music journalist and Richard got that erection again. He had his records, friends, papers, Dostoyevsky, and a dream of owning a decent secondhand record shop.

'. . . and I'll give you the address for *Fantastic Life* after this, another from our guests tonight: Yeah Yeah Noh.' Richard walked over to the dining table.

64

'Another magazine to send away for,' said The Kid. 'You've got an entire cupboardful through there already.'

'If somebody goes to the trouble of producing a magazine, I can go to the trouble of getting it. I mean if I don't want it,' Richard indicated his records, 'who's going to?'

'Most of these magazines are crap, though.'

'They're all right when they've got interviews with Pat Nevin, aren't they? And as you said earlier, I've got a wider range of appreciation than you.' Richard looked triumphant. 'I like getting things through the post. See when you send off for a record in America to some wee group and they send you back a letter, it's great. It really cheers me up.'

'All I ever get through the post is my giro,' said Archie.

'All I ever get is letters from Glasgow Rangers offering me a trial,' joked Mental.

'Yeah Yeah Noh,' said Peel, 'and their . . . er . . . classic, I suppose, "Cottage Industry". And the address for *Fantastic Life* is — picks up piece of paper, can't find piece of paper; ah, here it is — *Fantastic Life*, 18 Luckdale Drive — that's luck as in luck, dale as in dale — 18 Luckdale Drive, Wintombley — that's W-I-N-T-O-M-B-L-E-Y — Wintombley, the Isle of Man. That's *Fantastic Life*, 18 Luckdale Drive, Wintombley, Isle of Man. Don't think I've ever been to the Isle of Man. Anyway, this is Junior Byles.'

Richard noted the address straight onto an envelope and turned down the volume of the hi-fi.

'Put on *Newsnight*,' said Mental.

'No,' said Richard. 'If you choose television as your information supply then you limit your potential for understanding.'

'Come on. I just want to see the news, for fuck's sake. Let's see the big story. You know, somebody actually decides "the news". It's somebody's job.'

'And one Briton killed by a terrorist equals ten thousand Third World peasants killed in an earthquake,' said Richard. 'I hate the way *Newsnight* has these wee arty bits at the end. You know, a feature on a sculptor or a new film, something like that. It's just the same as the skateboarding budgie you get on the *News at 5.45*. I hate that.'

'Who are we going to get for the football?' asked Archie.

They spent the next five minutes deciding on ten names for the football: Davie, Mental, Richard, Archie, Bob Johnson, Wee Stevie, Charlie Whatsisname, Wayne Hughes (Mental: 'I hate him. He's a greedy bastard. He never passes the ball'), and Chas and Rab.

'If anybody doesn't turn up there's always plenty of guys in the conditioning room we can get to play,' said Mental.

'. . . and he said, "I don't know, John". Typical. Now this next record I first heard when a bunch of us were driving back to Dallas, Texas after a show in Houston. And this came on the radio, so I pulled over, stopped the car and we all cried. Ahhhhhh, those were the days. What twerps. Otis Redding, *Ole Man Trouble*. This one's for The Pig.'

'Turn it up,' said Mental. There was no need. Richard was already adjusting the volume. Throughout the land people stopped what they were doing and listened to Otis: kids in bed, people on the night shift, people like Archie.

'Haven't heard that for ages, Otis Redding, of course — I must stop saying "of course" — and *Ole Man Trouble*. And to conclude the story I was telling you beforehand, I should point out that the car wouldn't start afterwards. Serves you right for being bourgeois enough to have a car, I hear you cry. And you're probably right. Now another from tonight's guests, Yeah Yeah Noh: *Bias Binding*.'

'I hate all those wacky post-XTC groups with their puns and stupid names,' said Mental.

'Peel would say it's better to champion the new groups than just play the old favourites,' said Richard, 'or else you end up appreciating music for completely the wrong reasons. You see, you don't like Yeah Yeah Noh but you've never gone out of your way to listen to them; buy their records, whatever. Whereas you would buy REM because they project traditional values. They have reference points which you find comforting.'

Mental shook his head and said, 'That's garbage. Yeah Yeah Noh are garbage. This song mentions "putting the fun back into being pretentious". That's pathetic; so wacky, so student-like. You notice how Peel never plays REM, I don't like that. It's as if REM are some big rock band. And you prefer REM to that shower, don't you?'

'Of course, I'm just using Peel's argument. You see, he is now very embarrassed about a lot of the stuff he used to listen to, and with REM he adopts a "won't get fooled again/heard it all before" stance. It's too easy for the distant and vague to be idolised. It's like I used to be really in awe of hippies. They always looked aloof and superior — it must've been the drugs — and I used to think they represented what I wanted to be. No chance. They were really thick and really aggressive. I went to a few festivals, ma-a-an, and these hippies with their cheesecloth shirts and beads were really intimidating, physically intimidating.'

'That's what happens when you spend too much time outdoors,' said Mental.

'I was really nervous about talking music with the hippies. I was sure they would know so much more than me. Huh, some chance, they hadn't a clue about records.'

'Hence the expression "Never trust a hippy",' said Mental.

'The music they listened to was just Val Doonican for the pretentious: Gong, Yes, E-L-P' — each letter announced with revulsion — 'and Tangerine Dream. Mind Wee Stevie's big brother said that a Tangerine Dream LP had killed some lad over in Germany? He'd made the mistake of listening to it all the way through. You were only supposed to listen to one side a day!'

'That's right,' laughed Mental. 'One side was supposed to have the same effect as seven pints.' They all laughed.

When Mental and Richard argued about music, they agreed on everything within Mental's range of appreciation so Richard had to take the opposing point of view in order to prolong and make interesting, the debate.

'Peel doesn't like Springsteen either,' continued Richard. 'I remember there used to be this programme on Friday nights; a magazine/review show hosted by a guy called Michael Wale — he always used to say "Oh, ah, my name's Michael Wale" on his trailers, remember him? No. Well, anyway, Paul Gambaccini . . .'

'I hate Paul Gambaccini,' said Mental: 'that guy is a boring bastard. An *intensely* boring bastard.'

'. . . played this new record from America called *Born to Run* as a review record, and this guy Michael Wale had Peel on the programme to pass judgement on the so-called "future of rock and roll" and Peel dismisses it as pretentious crap and says "Give me the Floyd any day".' Richard's Peel quote had Mental rolling about the floor helpless with laughter. '"Give me the Floyd any day," dearie fucking dear.'

'It's the same with him wanting to be known by his surname,' continued Richard. 'That's very dodgy. It makes you think of Clapton, Page, Beck, Wakeman, Blackmore, Gillan, all manner of scum.'

'Emerson, Lake and Palmer,' said Archie.

'Exactly,' said Richard, enjoying the attention. 'All the greats are known by their Christian names: Bruce, Muddy, Buddy, Elvis, Chuck, Otis, Aretha, Smokey, Prince, all of them.'

'Sam and Dave,' offered Archie.

'How about Howlin' Wolf?' asked Mental, creating a puzzle.

'Howlin' Wolf was Howlin' Wolf,' answered Richard, eventually. 'I wish you'd stop trying to ruin my great theories, Mental.'

'So Peel should be known as John,' said Archie.

'Who else do you think of when you hear the name John?' asked Richard. There was silence for fully five seconds.

'Lennon?' said The Kid.

'No, he's Lennon,' said Richard. Mental nodded five times.

'John Lee Hooker?'

'Nah, he's John Lee Hooker.'

'I can't think of anybody called John,' said Archie wondering just how stupid he sounded while desperately trying to think of someone called John.

'So Peel's the definitive John,' said Mental.

'*John*,' said Richard.

John was back announcing Keith Hudson's awesome *Nah skin up*. 'Always goes down well at gigs that one. And I still can't find that request. How infuriating. Ah well, if it was you who stopped me on Saturday night and said "Hey fatso, what about *Nah Skin Up*, then that was for you. Sorry. And you can have this one as well, the new single from the Sisters of Mercy.'

'TURN IT OFF!' shrieked Mental. Richard likewise drew the line at the Sisters of Mercy and cut the volume.

'Davie still hate the work?' asked Richard.

'Loathes it,' said Mental. 'That big guy we seen earlier is going to start work with him tomorrow. Where's the "dignity of labour" in that shit, I ask you?'

'They want to increase the quantity of work by decreasing the quality,' said Richard. 'I was thinking of going round and cleaning everybody's windows for free, sweep up the streets, all that kind of stuff. Demonstrate freedom, and see how they liked it. Wonder what would happen? Be a laugh.'

'Do you know how people become Tories?' asked Mental. 'They convince themselves that they have *earned* their homes, their possessions and shit. You get Tory celebrities flaunting their wealth and telling us how hard they've worked to earn it. They actually equate their wealth with how hard they work. That's garbage. It's offensive.'

'It was the same with punk,' said Archie, 'all the old hippies talked about "paying your dues" and "musicianship". They said The Pistols couldn't play their instruments. They were just trying to justify their extravagance by claiming allegiance to the work ethic.' Archie would happily have sat all night listening to Richard and Mental. He didn't like contributing; he felt he was interrupting, and silence usually fell as everybody forgot what they were talking about. Richard turned up the radio.

'. . . what a twerp. I always fail to understand why it is that popular music — pop music, rock music, call it what you will — is the only art form for which one's appreciation is expected to diminish as one grows older. I simply cannot understand it. And if you know the answer, put it on a postcard and send it to that twerp. I don't know. I must confess I'd quite like to wake up tomorrow and discover I was a teapot. Here's The Fall. God bless them.'

'John should write his autobiography,' said Mental. 'I'd be well into that.'

'He doesn't suffer the same nostalgia trip as his contemporaries,' said Richard. 'The my-youth-was-better--than-your-youth-good-old-days shit. Although he does say that hearing rock 'n' roll for the first time was an experience no other generation would ever appreciate.'

'Hearing some records for the first time isn't always an accurate way to judge them,' said The Kid. He turned to Archie. 'Mind that track *Julia* by Pavlov's Dog?' Archie nodded. 'It was about eight years ago. Wee Stevie's big brother gave us a loan of this LP. It was really great. But that track *Julia* was unbelievable. It's not as if I had crap taste at the time or anything, but nowadays when I hear it, it sounds okay. Just okay. I used to love it with a passion.'

'I've got the two Pavlov's Dog LPs,' said Richard. 'Some records have the completely opposite effect. When the first Swell Maps LP came out, I didn't rate it too much, but for the past couple of weeks I've been playing it all the time. It's funny how the art school end of punk never dated the same way the working-class groups did. I suppose they were fuelled by influence rather than imitation.'

'Best to be fuelled by inspiration,' said Mental, 'like Paul McStay.'

Archie looked at Richard sitting cross-legged on the floor. He was dressed as he had been earlier, minus the Levi jacket. His hair was extremely untidy.

'How come you call me a scruff when he goes about looking like that?' Archie asked Mental.

'Ah, that's designer scruff. You're the real thing. Let me explain. Designer scruff doesn't go around covered in mud, neither does it go about with three days growth when you can't grow a beard.' Mental tickled Archie's hairy neck: 'Designer scruff is relaxed and contemplative, you're lazy and gawkit. Dirt is never trendy, muchacho.'

'At least he hasn't mentioned your BO,' said Richard.

'That's one thing I can't stand about Archie; the amount of talc he puts on. He stinks of the stuff.'

'What am I supposed to say to that?' queried Archie. 'Forget it. I'm not bothered.'

'A-ha,' said Richard. 'That's apathy talking.'

'You should . . .,' started Mental.

'I've told you to stop saying that,' said Archie. 'It always ends up with me doing something to make myself more like you.'

'That's one thing I don't like about wearing tracksuit bottoms outdoors,' said Richard, 'they promote body smells in the nether regions. You never feel fresh.'

'What do you mean?' said Mental interested. 'Like you've pissed yourself?'

'Sort of. Not really. More dirty.'

'Crapped yourself?' suggested Archie.

'NO,' roared Richard. 'Just dirty in a sort of . . . Oh, forget it.'

'Like wearing pyjamas outdoors,' Archie tried again.

'Yeah, that's it. All the dogs want a good sniff.'

'Why wear them outdoors then?' enquired Mental.

'Cause they make me look really skinny, of course.'

'. . . and I was listening to this over the weekend and it sounded pretty darn good. Excellent, in fact. *Midget Submarines* from Swell Maps.'

'You were just on about that,' exclaimed Mental. 'What a coincidence. Pretty freaky, in point of fact. Weird. There's something going on. I don't like this. We need to smoke some more shit . . . I have decided.'

'You have decided,' said Richard.

'I have decided. And since the Hun's not here I'm going to have to roll it cause you two are useless. Mine might not be as good as the Hun's but they're better than yours . . . I have decided.'

Nine

'Funny. You were talking earlier about hearing records for the first time.' Mental passed the shit to Richard after having had a few draws. 'There are girls like that. There's this lassie that moved in down the road a few weeks ago. And the first time I saw her I thought she was the most beautiful woman in the world.' There was sadness in Mental's voice. 'But after that all I could see was flaws. I always want to go up to her and tell her that one day I thought she was the most beautiful woman in the world.' Mental shook his head as if troubled by guilt.

'You wanting the boxing on, Archie?' asked Richard.

'It's okay. My dad's taping it as well. I'll get plenty of time to study it.'

'Do you fancy coming through to Edinburgh next week?' asked Richard.

'Yeah, sure,' enthused Archie. A day in Edinburgh. Magic.

'No,' said The Kid. 'I hate Edinburgh. Full of Americans and Hearts supporters.'

On childhood holidays, The Mental Kid would be physically sick in boarding house toilets, such was his discomfiture at being away from home. Daily, he would phone home to Archie and Davie, pronouncing himself suicidally bored with Scarborough, Blackpool, Great Yarmouth (twice) and, eventually, Majorca. The last named took place when The Sex Pistols' *Holidays in the Sun* was released. The line about 'cheap holidays in other people's misery' summed up Majorca. And so Mental became the ultimate home bird; locked in the cage and nailed to the perch. Only following Celtic took him away from home — and he truly loathed away matches: 'Tannadice is a fucking dump!' etc. The last (non-football) excursion to Edinburgh was to see the Pope. He was forced to go.

'What are you reading just now?' Archie asked Richard.

'Bernard Malamud, *The Tenant*. It's okay. He's Jewish and that serves as a lot of the punchlines.'

'I don't like those people who make a living by taking the piss out of their culture,' said Mental. 'Like when you get Irish comedians or intellectuals going on about being Irish. I hate that. When you get a black celebrity on the telly and somebody makes a joke about their skin colour, they have to laugh. They have to . . . comply.'

'I agree,' said Richard handing the joint to Archie.'If they got up and walked out the media would infer that black people were petulant. That they were paranoid and uptight.'

'You should see Davie's dad when there's some guy on the telly like Jim Davidson. He pisses himself. There's a kind of . . .' Mental struggled for the word, 'aggression in his laughter. It frightens me.'

'Mind he went daft when we watched Richard Pryor,' said Archie.

'I know,' said Mental. 'Pryor was so fucking cool. Davie's dad sat and watched it for half an hour then he goes, "That's not true. White people aren't like that. When I did my National Service it was them that were frightened of the snakes." Fucking hell, what a fascist. He really upset me.' Mental shook his head. 'Another thing he does is to forget black people's names, sportsmen and that. And see when they're called McGregor or something like that, he always has a smug little grin on his face.'

'You still reading Simenon?' Richard asked Archie.

'Yeah. *The Iron Staircase*. I think it's his best.'

'I don't like reading books,' said Mental. 'You're so aware when you're reading the book that you're never going to read it again. That moment will never be repeated. And it's not as if the moment is so special that you're going to recall it for all eternity. I find it depressing. Books reinforce your mortality.' Mental stared at Richard, challenging the bookworm to disagree.

'It's strange you should say that. Recently, I've become increasingly aware that when I read books I'll never be reading them again. It's not like records where the pleasure derives from repeated listening. I feel that way about my papers as well. When I first started buying *NME* I used to pore over it; read it three times a week, you know, and I was always looking back at them. But now I buy it, read it from cover to cover then put it in the cupboard. I don't have the time to look back over them. I always look forward to them, like. I'm just getting old I suppose.'

'That's why records are best,' said Mental. 'They don't reinforce your mortality. The Stooges are immortal!'

Grinderswitch's *Pickin' the Blues* signalled the end of another John Peel show. John apologised for talking too much and promised that the next show would be a cracker. Just you wait and see.

The midnight news summary contained a report about a vicious sex attack.

'Those scum should be strung up,' said Richard.

'You want to hang everybody,' said Mental. 'If just one person gets wrongly convicted then the whole system is discredited.'

Richard shook his head. 'The penal system as it stands cannot prevent the convicted from reoffending upon release. Nobody ever questions that.'

Archie could never understand Richard's support for the death penalty. The arguments were cogent and thought through but it seemed the antithesis of Richard's lifestyle to be so clinical.

'You see,' continued Richard, 'I believe too many criminals are unaware of the damage they cause, how much they upset people. Say, for example, some guy stole my record collection. Now I make no bones about the fact I've got them insured and I dare say I would enjoy building up a new collection. I would be bloody upset though. Likewise, if some drunk driver ran down Dostoyevsky, I'd quite like to see some sort of punishment dished out. They've got no respect. They are people who conduct themselves in such a manner that they can be called evil.'

'Oh, come on,' said Mental. 'That's a bit strong.'

'The word exists,' Richard leaned forward, 'and it defines certain intentions. Everybody has an opinion on evil. Some say Hitler was evil, some say Idi Amin was evil, or Ian Paisley is evil. Trouble is these people had quite a few followers. But I think their callousness and their actions could be described as evil. I believe the right — the racist right — are evil. People who commit sex crimes are evil. Understand what I'm getting at? I find it strange that if any such attack occurred to a member of your family you would be willing to act out personal revenge but you wouldn't be willing to endorse the legislation of such actions.'

Archie handed the joint to Mental and the latter tutted at the sopping roach before saying, 'I see what you're getting at but look . . . I don't know why people commit sex crimes, I really don't. I've heard guys saying that so-and-so would be worth a few years away. They're just joking, it's their way. I've heard guys talking about women in a way that frightens me. I just assume that these attackers are sad, lonely, unfulfilled wee men. They must suffer a lot in order to be so callous. Maybe it's suppressed guilt. If they just stopped and had a wank there would be no trouble and they'd have a good time in the process. I don't think it's their fault, the way they are. I don't think they're evil. I'm afraid I feel sorry for them.' Mental was unused to playing the liberal.

'Evil,' said Richard. 'It exists, therefore define it.'

'Off the top of my head, I can't. But a lot of things look worse when you describe them subjectively. Like there are some people we know that others would regard as racist because they use the word "nigger" and they make jokes about black people.'

'THAT IS FUCKING RACIST!' Richard was getting angry. 'This is my point, entirely. That is how I define a racist. When

I was at university, I got on really well with this guy I later discovered was a member of the National Front. I'm not saying that because somebody is a racist then it is completely impossible to get on with them. That's the bloody trouble, it's the exact opposite. It's like Davie's dad; he knows his football, doesn't he? You can have good rants about football. He's an Orangeman, you're a Catholic.'

'I don't like the way that Chas and Rab say "nigger" all the time, but I don't believe they're racist.'

'Who are the racists then?'

'I don't know,' Mental was looking depressed.

'Glasgow Rangers supporters? Chelsea supporters? Anything distant and obvious; different and obvious. The left take a media slagging because they see racism in everything — nursery rhymes, whatever. But how come people can accept other changes in their lives, in the way they live and things like that, but you cannot see the harm done by assessments made by skin colour.'

'See, you're making me out to be a racist now because I don't believe in the death penalty! This is stupid. I think you're a very intelligent person and you've changed the way I think about a lot of things but I don't believe in the death penalty. I just don't.'

'In any vision of the future: books, films, science fiction, whatever — there is always a termination lab, a zapping chamber. You cannot perceive the future without seeing the death penalty. A place where you "do in" evil bastards.'

'Science fiction never refers to Catholicism, football and a million other things that will never go away. It's not a reliable guide to future trends. Look, over the years a lot of people have hurt me, really hurt me. And they've got away with it. There was nothing I could do, or say, that would in any way make me feel better. I've lost sleep and I've lost friends. But it happens to everybody. I don't become all self-righteous about it and start saying that because I lead a decent life those who don't should be strung up. You've had a lot of advantages in your life, Richard.'

'Eh? You're saying that I believe in the death penalty because Susan left. You're the one making ridiculous connections now.'

'I never mentioned her.'

'You implied pretty heavily.'

Archie turned to Mental and said, 'He's always been in favour of the death penalty. It's because his beloved Julie Burchill says that Labour would win the next election if it went for the law and order vote.'

'They probably would,' said Richard with a smile.

'Who decides who hangs who?' asked Mental. 'Domestic murders? The ideologically sound terrorist?'

'These are different areas of debate, separate arguments. Does putting people in prison ease your conscience?'

'Of course not. But hanging is not a deterrent.'

'I don't use the deterrent argument. Maybe there are times when it's suitable punishment.'

'And what would be suitable punishment for this guy that nicked your record collection, or the drunk driver that ran over Dostoyevsky?' asked Archie.

'Well, drunk drivers that cause fatalities should, in my opinion, be put in jail for ten years minimum. Of course with a dog they'll probably be let off. As for theft . . . look, it's not up to me to decide these things. If you want me to come up with an answer I'd need to think about it.'

They sat in silence for a few minutes. Richard went through to the kitchen to make some tea and toast.

'That shit was crap,' said Mental biting into his toast.

'It wasn't very good,' said Richard. 'I'm not taking any more deals off Stevie.' He went over to the record player and put on Joe Gibbs' *African Dub Chapter Two* very quietly.

They always had good rants, Mental and Richard. The miners' strike provided eighteen months of debating material. Mental was completely disillusioned with the Protestant work ethic and found the refusal to hold a ballot smug and disturbing. Richard blamed the miners' loss on their amateurish use of the media and the media's innate bias. He talked of camera angles, interview locations and distorted emphasis. A ballot was useless, Richard said, since the media determined the information supply and the media was biased. The miners had elected leaders to make decisions on their behalf. That's what Scargill's job was. But Mental was unimpressed. The miners represented everything he hated

77

about the 'mince and tatties mentality': 'All these places are Hun cities. Take Bo'ness, for example, typical fucking mining community. Hun bastards. You've got all these fat bastards moaning about not having any food. And I hate the word "scab". People degrade themselves by using that kind of attack.' They all wanted to see the miners win and they all agreed that Leonard Parkin was a fascist. But mostly they wanted to see Margaret Hilda Thatcher melt.

Archie loved his nights up at Richard's: the records, the blethers, sometimes a video, a bottle of cider and a packet of biscuits nicked by Mental. When Mental talked intelligently, Archie felt a certain pride. With Richard you expected reasoned argument because of his academic background and his reading. The Mental Kid seldom read anything and at times was sullen and uncommunicative. A lot of people thought Mental was thick and said so behind his back, but they only ever saw him when he was drunk, when all he talked about was football and chasing women. Archie felt like Mental's mistress when they went to Richard's.

Richard walked over to the window and surveyed the landscape. 'I'm always last to go to bed,' he declared. 'The doctor told me to get to bed before twelve and get up before nine. I go to bed at two and get up at eight.' He laughed.

'It's been a funny day,' said Archie. 'We've done a lot.'

'We have,' agreed Mental. 'And Davie says he's going out for a bev tomorrow.' Mental shook his head. 'I don't know if I can afford it. I've got a fiver for my weekend partying and that's it till my next giro. My sister'll maybe buy me a drink.'

'I quite fancy going out tomorrow myself,' said Richard. 'It's been a while since we all went out for a drink. Does Terasa still hate me?'

'She doesn't hate you,' said Mental. 'It's just that she cannot understand your way of life.'

'I'd quite like the life she's got: steady relationship, looking forward to starting a marriage and a family. All that shit.'

'I know what you mean,' said Mental. 'See last Christmas I was really fucked up. You know why? I decided it was because I didn't have any kids. I desperately wanted to give them bicycles and Celtic strips. I wanted to see Brendan and Patrick with their Celtic strips and Terasa with her bike.'

Christmas for Archie meant getting games but having no one to play them with. It meant big plates and trifle; the only three-course meal of the year.

'Just think,' said Richard, 'Davie and Terasa are in bed. Two people who are in love. Tomorrow they're going to wake up and see each other. That was what it used to be like with me and Susan. It was great. It was the best.'

'You're well rid of her,' said Mental. 'Records are better.'

'That's the thing, I'm actually happier up here with my records, playing them all day. Fucking magic. That's as good as life gets. These little bursts of Nirvana. But it's so fucking selfish. I need to give.'

'You can give me a fiver,' suggested Mental. 'I've got a very appreciative smile.'

'I don't know what it is.'

'You need to stop feeling sorry for yourself.'

'I know. I can be really good at that. Why do you get suicidal about the most stupid things? When Susan left I wasn't suicidal, but when she never sent me a birthday card I was.'

'You don't see enough of people. You don't see *their* problems. Archie's the same. The pair of you spend the bulk of your time keeping yourselves to yourselves. Too much time to brood. Don't take this as an insult, but you're the two most fucked up people I know. I'm never alone, there's always someone there.'

Archie wanted to light a cigarette and say the word 'obviously' but he refrained.

Mental continued: 'You don't appreciate how much you're loved, by your folks and that. Everybody always asks for you. Sometimes it's pretty hard coming up with things to say about youse. I agree that listening to records is as good as life gets but you can do other things that make you feel good: chasing women, getting drunk and arguing about football.'

It was twenty past one.

'Well, are we breezing then?' Mental asked Archie.

'Yeah; suppose so,' said Archie. 'I've really enjoyed tonight.'

'This is as good as life gets,' said Richard.

'I'll come round for you tomorrow night,' said Archie. 'We'll meet the rest of them down the pub.'

'Okay,' said Richard. 'See you in time for *Top of the Pops*.'

When Mental and Archie reached the bottom of the stairs they saw that the front door had been kicked in. There was glass everywhere.

'Funny guy, Richard,' said Mental. 'You don't see him for ages and then he pops up and you realise you're his best friend. It's a burden I don't like.'

'You mean he leeches on to you?'

'Not really. I like him a lot. I think he's great. But I don't like him slagging off Chas and Rab, he hardly knows them.'

'I think he's that much above everybody around here. He's not a smalltown person. He'd be happier in London.'

'He would. But he says he'd be leading the same lifestyle down there so he's as well to stay here. I think he'd be happier with a career but he says there's no integrity in that.'

Archie pointed to a row of terraced flats. 'See the guy-that-never-talks-to-us is still up. What does he do at this time of night?'

'Short-wave radio. He's a great lad. Knows more about football than anyone I know. He's got some fucking knowledge, I'll tell you. He's got tons of hobbies.'

They walked the rest of the way in silence before saying goodnight.

Archie got home to find some pieces in the bread bin and he poured himself a glass of milk. It was two o'clock when he got to bed. He felt very tired but he could not get to sleep. The last time he remembered looking at his watch it was quarter past three.

Archie had a nightmare about being on holiday in Carnoustie. In his company were his friends and family. Archie became detached from them and wandered over the golf course. Holidaymakers were sunbathing on the golf course.

Nobody was playing golf. There was a big building like a town hall or a church with a bell tower. Archie saw a vicious-looking skinhead enter the building. Six of his skinhead friends stood silent at the foot of the building, looking up. They looked similarly hard. Two of them were girls. Archie saw the skinhead at the top of the building. The skinhead dived off and hit the deck with a dull thud. One of the girls jogged over to a phonebox while another removed her jacket and placed it over the dead youth's head. Archie ran through the golf course to get back to his friends. Nobody was interested, though. Mental said, 'So what', and licked his ice-cream. Archie looked back to the skinheads. They stood motionless, calm with their thoughts.

Archie woke at ten past five, went to the toilet and emptied his bladder. He stood at the side of the urinal as he always did, wondering if anybody else peed that way. He smiled to himself.

Ten

Seven forty-two. Magic. Archie felt lovely. It was worth going through the horror of sleeplessness and nightmares to feel this good. Only his forehead was exposed to the air. Archie was barely conscious. I could go to sleep any second. Why can't it always be so easy? Archie fell asleep again.

At twenty past nine, he reawoke and felt rotten. His head felt scrambled. The chorus and verse of *Pride* ran through his head simultaneously. Archie lit a cigarette and proceeded to dress, donning the same clothes as he had been wearing for the past three days. The nicotine creating routine, he made a plan: wash, breakfast, change sheets and pillow-cases, have a bath, change clothes, dinner, then walk down to the library. Changing the sheets meant he wouldn't have to make the bed just now. He always slept better in fresh sheets.

Archie drew the curtains and looked out of the window. Theirs was the only garden with flowers, a hut and a greenhouse. His dad did all the physical work and his mum kept it tidy. Most of the neighbours were younger than Archie. They never appeared to go out. Their lights always remained on.

Archie finished his cigarette and stubbed it out in the dessert plate that functioned as an ashtray.

In the bathroom he washed his face and brushed his teeth. Shaving was still too much like hard work — maybe after he'd had his bath. Archie brushed his teeth twice a day and made biannual trips to the dentist. The DHSS paid for any treatment. False teeth and naked gums filled him with dread. He brushed with vigour to compensate for his smoking. Richard had terrible teeth. He claimed they were as smart as Keith Richards' but Mental said they were as bad as Bowie's. After watching an episode of *That's Life* wherein Esther Rantzen investigated dental payments and discovered that different dentists gave different estimates to the same patients, Richard had never been back to a dentist. He didn't like the idea of unnecessary work being carried out by sterile, sexless fingers.

The cabinet mirror showed lines around Archie's eyes. These lines would never go away but would grow longer, darker and thicker. Archie could stare in the mirror for hours. He hated standing beside somebody, though, it always made him feel ugly. But on his own he thought he looked okay. By adjusting the doors of the cabinet he could get a picture of what he really looked like. Initial reaction was always revulsion. Nobody's *that* ugly. It was nothing like the picture he carried around in his head. Archie tried smiling and frowning, wondering which looked coolest. Years spent staring at the mirror had revealed nothing. He suspected, as Mental said, that he looked gawkit.

Funny how I always wash before I brush my teeth, Archie thought. I mean common sense dictates I should do the opposite. I'm going to have to rinse toothpaste off my face, anyway. Who taught me this?

'Morning.' Archie addressed his mother in the living-room. She was doing the *Daily Record* crossword.

'What's a nine-letter words for "deny"? Something E and it ends A something E.' She sucked a pen.

AE, BE, CE, DE, EE, FE, GE, gelignite, germinate, NO! HE
hesitate, IE, JE, KE, LE, levitate, ME. Deny, deny you're such
a liar, Archie sang the Clash song to himself. NE, OE, PE, QE,
RE — I like that, yeah, RE, RE, eh . . . 'Repudiate!'

'That's it. And that'll be Madeira. I finished the crossie.
Heh, heh.' Archie's mum flung the paper on to the settee.

Archie filled a large soup plate with Wheetaflakes and
drowned them in three-quarters of a pint of milk and
walked over to the settee. Archie was an untidy eater.
He had to gulp twice before inserting another mouth-
ful.

'What was Auntie Isabel saying?' Archie asked.

'She got a phone call while we were there from Joan
saying that my Uncle George is in hospital in Kirkcaldy.
We're maybe going to take a run up and see him. See how
your dad feels.'

'When was he taken in?' Archie knew nothing of Uncle
George apart from the fact that he was old, sent a Christmas
card and Archie's mum and dad saw him at funerals.

'I don't know. I think it was Monday. They fairly took
their time in telling folk.' Archie's mum sounded disappointed.

Archie turned the pages of the *Daily Record* while
devouring his breakfast. The TV page, cartoon page and
the sports page were studied the most.

'If you spill any milk on that settee, I'll kill you,' said
Archie's mum, only quarter joking. She lit a cigarette as
Archie read the latest adventures of his personal guru:
Bogart, the cat in the *Roz* cartoon strip.

Archie finished his cereal as his mother finished her cigarette. She took his plate through to the kitchen while singing
My Love is like a Red, Red Rose. Archie read the sports
pages. It was so easy to keep up with the world of sport
without actually bothering about it, especially football. It
always seemed strange to Archie that those people of his
acquaintance who could talk about football till 'all the
seas gang dry, my love' weren't very gifted footballers
themselves. Richard was a better player than Mental and
Davie but he couldn't tell you the manager of Hearts. He
said he played football to keep skinny.

The report of the Hagler fight was dull, like describing sex without adjectives. The latest Rangers crisis, though, really got the journalists worked up. Did they get worked up about Rangers' sectarianism? Did they hell, they got worked up about Rangers' poor form. Every so often the papers would act the liberal by making a fuss about some aspect of Rangers' policy: 'Rangers player marries Catholic . . . Rangers sign Catholic schoolboy on S-form'. Following the last story, the Celtic fans sang 'What's it like to sign a Pape?' at the next Old Firm game. Journalists, MPs and publicity seekers never sought to campaign for civil rights at Ibrox for fear of the backlash. Even terrorists shunned it.

Quarter past ten, near enough. Archie's mother would be leaving for her school dinners work at eleven.

The smell of stale tobacco stunned Archie as he entered his room. What a dump! There were records, cassettes, magazines, dirty clothes and books all over the place. The colour of the room was nicotine yellow. The poster of Jimi Hendrix looked like his corpse. Other pictures were of Frank Bruno, Barry McGuigan, Bono, Kenny Dalglish (in Celtic colours), Prince, Marc Bolan and there were four of Marvin Hagler. The biggest poster advertised SPOT (Sex Pistols On Tour) which Archie bought off Wee Stevie for two pounds. The white background on the poster was now yellow.

As well as his double bed and his music centre the room contained two fitted wardrobes, an upright chair and a chest of drawers. One fitted wardrobe was packed with Archie's old papers and records (Archie had two hundred LPs and three hundred singles. He considered this amount tiny compared to Richard's) and the other contained his clothes, games and school stuff, which had never been thrown out. The top drawer of Archie's chest of drawers contained Archie's cassettes. Archie spent fully five minutes deciding what to play when changing the bed. He narrowed it down to a choice of *NME*'s *Pocket Jukebox* and *The Cream of Al Green*. He chose Al Green. Richard had given Archie the recording about a year previous. Whereas The Mental Kid ransacked Richard's records for things to tape, Archie was always happy with whatever Richard taped for him. Richard had introduced Archie to Bobby

Bland, the Neville Brothers, Lee Perry, Laura Nyro, David Ackles, Hüsker Dü, lots of reggae and funk, and most recently Tim Buckley and Nick Drake. In truth, Richard was not entirely happy at lending out records to Archie who only had a cheap music centre which could have damaged Richard's records. Archie expressed his gratitude in terms of enthusiasm and interest.

Archie pulled the covers off the bed: five blankets, two sheets and a tartan bed cover. All punctured with cigarette burns. There was an eight-year-old stain on the mattress where Archie had been sick. He had hoped the stain would have disappeared over the years. No such luck. He always intended to invert the mattress so that the stain would be unseen but he never got round to it.

In the airing cupboard, Archie got fresh sheets and pillow-cases.

Al Green sang *Here I Am*. Awesome. Archie turned up the volume and opened the window, giving thanks to the inspiration that made him select that tape. Although he'd have enjoyed most of his collection as much. Next up was *Unchained Melody*. Archie had never associated that title with that song. It had been the same when he'd discovered that Booker T's *Soul Limbo* was the music they used to introduce cricket on television. Next was *I Stand Accused*. Archie had another version of this on a Stax compilation by Isaac Hayes.

'Well, I'm away then.' Archie's mum stuck her head through the door. She looked as if her nose was being stuck into a pair of underpants that hadn't been washed for three weeks. 'Put the sheets and that in the basket. This place needs decorating, you know.'

'Yeah,' said Archie. 'As soon as I've left you can do what you like.' Archie was smiling. There was a greater likelihood of Nelson leaving his column.

'By the way, your Aunt Isabel was talking to Wilma Stevenson. She was asking for you. Asking if you had a job yet.' Archie's mum was wearing her hurt expression which made Archie's neck swell. She did this every so often. It hurt. He reasoned that he could be a lot worse: into drugs or crime, away from home, dead. It didn't work.

Archie found it difficult to appreciate that he was the most important person in her life. It was something he didn't like thinking about.

'Right, cheerio. I'll see you later. There's cold meat in the fridge.'

Archie said, 'Okay, cheerio.' He wanted to say something else, something personal. He didn't. He never did. He turned up the volume for Al Green's version of *I Can't Get Next To You* while wondering whether anyone had ever made a bed while listening to Al Green before.

His mother waved as she walked past the window. She made a funny face and then relaxed into a smile. Archie blew her a kiss and she blew one back.

The bed was made. It looked good, great even. Archie knew he would sleep well tonight. The tape finished.

Archie played a 12" single of Smokey Robinson's *And I Don't Love You* while he did his hundred sit-ups (securing his feet under the chest of drawers) hundred press-ups and hundred knee bends. He lit a cigarette when he finished and flexed his skinny muscles.

Quarter past eleven. Bath time. Archie selected a pair of red underpants, a pair of white socks and a white T-shirt to change into after his bath. While he ran the bathwater he played Hüsker Dü's *Eight Miles High*.

Archie liked his baths very hot. He liked to lie there for a couple of hours until the water got cold then he washed himself. Once he weighed himself before and after a bath and discovered he had lost two pounds in weight. While the bath was filling, Archie kneeled at the side of the tub and washed his hair. The family always bought its shampoo from the man who came round selling goods on behalf of the blind.

Waking up when you don't have to get up, listening to Al Green, having a good soak in a bath. Ahhhhhhhh.

Half past twelve. Archie cut his hair and shaved after his bath. He cut his hair with a cheap plastic trimmer. Usually he left bald patches. Today, though, he managed to get his hair good and short and tidy. He dried himself then cleaned the tub using a cloth which he found on the S-bend of the toilet. He opened the window to let the steam out. Before dressing he applied talc sparingly, recalling Mental's comment from the previous evening. He put his dirty clothes and towel into the, now full, wash basket.

Archie switched on the radio in the living-room to listen to James Sanderson's sportsdesk. Sanderson made football interesting. His Saturday evening phone-ins were great and Archie never missed them. The wee man that would never be caught 'sitting on the fence' and predicted cup draws with ease delivered his report.

For dinner Archie grilled the cold meat and tomato and served it with a healthy dollop of pickle. He opened a tin of fruit and served some of it with ice-cream. Four digestive biscuits and a glass of milk completed the meal.

Once finished, he washed the dishes and tidied the kitchen.

'Shit,' said Archie when he got back into the bedroom. In the middle of the floor lay the world's dirtiest pair of boots. Archie looked out the window. Brainwave! He officially declared it summertime. He would put the boots away and wear his slip-ons. Archie smiled at his genius. He put on the fourth side of *London Calling* and searched out the shoes. They were dirty but not filthy like the boots. An application of polish would clean them up. Hell, they were wipe-clean, even better.

I could do with some new clothes, Archie said to himself, while studying his wardrobe. A new jacket for sure and a couple of new shirts. Richard said it was always best to buy clothes that were slightly too big for you.

Archie considered his jackets: a blue cagoule (filthy and crumpled), a brown parka (horrible colour, thirteen years old), a dark grey dress jacket (far too small) and a grey overcoat. Archie put on the coat. It was far too big. The sleeves hid his knuckles. He had bought it eighteen months ago and only worn it three times. Nobody had said it was too big for him, in fact Mental had said it was a 'smart coat'. Archie studied himself in front of his parents' full-length mirror. Maybe it's not too big. Yes it is! Is it? The Undertones always wore clothes that were too small for them; it was Spandau Ballet that introduced baggy clothes. Archie turned up the collar and struck a few poses. Another brainwave. If

I can discard my boots I can go without a jacket. I'll put on my big, black jumper instead. Before putting on the jumper Archie tried on his old grey jacket. It reeked of stale tobacco. Between '79 and '83 Archie had worn this jacket every day. He'd worn it to every gig he'd ever been to. The lapels were ruined by the application of badges. It was the classic Undertones jacket. Archie removed it and put on his big, black jumper. With the big, black jumper he felt like a gangster's violin case, his muscles concealed by its bulk.

Archie skanked along to *Revolution Rock*. 'Doodoo doodoo doodoo doodoo doodoo doodoo doodoo./This here Revolution Rock.' He resolved to play *Get Over You* once *London Calling* was finished. The Undertones came from a culture where whistling and blowing bubble-gum stood for machismo. (Mental was the fiercest whistler.) Archie found the single in the haven't-been-played-for-a-while box.

Feargal's legendary whistle commenced *Get Over You*. The pretty boy pop stars never sang about getting dumped. Archie did a pogo: pledging allegiance to the flag, the punky, punky flag. He recalled seeing The Undertones live (three times). Feargal came on in parka and polo neck but was soon bare-chested. Archie was sure he pogoed higher than anyone else. Davie danced like a hip rhino and Mental danced part Soul Train show-off part Soweto defiance. The Blues Brothers on *Irn-bru*. They danced from the toes up, keeping all the joints in motion. Fuck shifting your weight from one foot to the other, this was dancing. Fuck steps and routines, this was dancing.

'I DON'T WANNA GET OVER YOU!' Awesome.

Archie collected his watch, keys, matches and cigarettes. He took a fiver from a coffee jar that served as a bank and crammed everything into his pockets.

The estate was quiet. A few women wearing jogging suits and pushing prams. The two signposts at the exit of the estate read Glasgow 25 miles and Edinburgh 25 miles. Some wag had added 'Caracus 8000 miles' to the Glasgow sign and 'Aids City' to the Edinburgh one.

An electric blue council van with a nuclear free zone sticker sped past Archie. There were millions of council vans. Archie wondered if Davie was in that van then chastised himself for 'playing the detective'. This was what his father did all the time. When his father drove past a house where he knew the occupant his hand would move in preparation of tooting the horn just in case somebody appeared at the window. Logie Baird Drive was bloody dangerous: he knew five people that stayed there.

Archie was increasingly wrong when 'playing the detective'. New shirt? Had it for ages. Seen you down the town? Wasn't down the town. Your sister work in *Low's*? Don't have a sister. Oh, fuck. He was wrong about the outcome of films, sport and relationships. He was taking life for granted but things didn't work that way.

Eleven

Is that Dostoyevsky running over there? Nah, it's a Dobermann but it's too ugly. Look, there's nothing wrong with keeping an eye out for a friend when you walk through the park. I've met Richard a few times walking through the park. He probably wouldn't recognise me without my jacket and boots and sporting a crucial haircut. Of course he would. I always look the same. How come I notice more about people than they notice about me? People don't notice me. If I was in a group I'd be the bass guitarist; really boring and my name is on the tip of your tongue. 'Doodoo doodoo doodoo doodoo doodoo doodoo doodoo/This here Revolution Rock.' Oh, stop feeling so sorry for yourself. Look, there's the Blind Hunt out for a walk. Go on, straight into a lamppost. It's incongruous being a blind hun. I bet he's a racist, too. I suppose you get thalidomide victims that are racist. I wonder what he thinks about. I mean do these guys actually think about offside decisions? Does Mental think about Peter Grant and Willie McStay? I've never thought about football in my life. People don't think about what they talk about. I wonder if Richard's spoken to anyone today. He says he only goes out in the morning to walk Dostoyevsky, so I suppose he hasn't. Mental was right about me spending too

much time on my own. He's never on his own. It's like
when we were kids we always had friends to go and see. No
time to think, too busy doing. I never thought about anything when I was a wee boy . . . apart from death. Nothing-
ness. I bet Mental never had that problem. Too busy.
And now I exist solely within my head: happy, sad, morning,
night, I'm in here all the time. This is the shit they call life.
How come I never explode? The burden of existence should
be mathematically impossible. The amount of information
and hassle that's in my brain — I should have konked
out by now. If I was Prince Edward I'd be cool: I'd walk
hand in hand with Winnie Mandela through the streets
of Soweto; I'd set up a chain of cinemas to show all the hip
films; I'd appear on *Whistle Test* choosing my favourite
records; I'd have a massive record collection gleaned
from all the cheap singles boxes in London (never taking
advantage of my title to secure gratuities); I'd get on the
cover of *NME*, the interview would be great, I'd slag off
everybody, especially the fascists; I'd make a film with
Prince (I wouldn't appear in it, maybe just a cameo, supporting role, equal billing. We'd remake *The Blues Brothers*.
Yeah); I'd organise massive charity events; I'd spar with
boxers and annoy the liberals (I'd rather be respected
by Marvin Hagler than Terry Wogan); I'd have an alternative
(God, I hate that word) Royal Variety Show, getting The
Pistols, The Velvet Underground and The Undertones to
reform. God, Prince Edward's wasted on that twerp!!
There's blue-and-yellow! Oh, God, I love you. Is she
walking my way? No. Shit, I forgot this is her day for
signing on. Has she noticed me? God, you're beautiful.
If I'd went down the town earlier I would maybe have
bumped into you. Mind that time I bumped into you on
Princes Street. Oh, God, I'm going to kill myself. She was
smiling. She was on her own. She was smiling because she
seen a familiar face . . . ME! God, what a prick. I was so
shy I pretended not to notice her. Her smile vanished and
she walked straight past. Oh God, I'm going to kill myself.
I upset her. I should've smiled, I should have said hello,
should've asked if she fancied a drink, fancied going up
Walter Scott's monument, fancied . . . Why am I such a

prick? I wonder if she knows my surname? I know hers and the middle ones. I know her birthday and her phone number (I overheard it once and that was it memorised for life. I never thought to look it up at any time.) I know the names of about twenty guys she's been out with. At school I knew every (outer) garment of clothing she owned, I know she went to Paisley College of Technology. I went daft when I saw your wedding photo in the paper. (He was fucking bald!) And I didn't breathe for two and a half hours when I was told that you were getting divorced and that you were back with your mam. And I've never even spoken to you. That does it, I'm going to kill myself. Is that Dostoyevsky? NO! 'Doodoo doodoo doodoo doodoo doodoo doodoo doodoo.' I wonder what my neighbours think about me? They must hear me. They must have formed opinions. Blue-and-yellow must have an opinion of me. Not necessarily. There are people I don't have an opinion of, specifically those people whose surnames I don't know. What did blue-and-yellow think on Princes Street? She certainly reacted to my presence. 'I love you/I love you.' Thank you, Aretha. Why did that song come into my head? Oh, you poor council workers. God, you look thick. Calm down. Stop being such a snob, for Christ's sake. If the exact same people were filmed in an office cradling a phone, holding a pen and watching a VDU would they look any smarter? Depends if they still had the tattoos. It's a Tory plot. Get the working class to look apathetic, give them jobs where you have to stand, give them oversized boilersuits, make available absolutely useless things for them to pilfer — bottles of sauce, rubber bands and specialised cleaners. Calm down. Calm down. What *was* that wee hut? It always gets Mental's goat to see 'Welcome to Parkhead' above the door. It's covered in Hun graffiti: 'No surrender', 'No Pope in Logie Baird Drive', 'Ulster 1690', all that shit. It's as if that hut was just put there as a canvas for Hun graffiti. It's like that road surface with all that shit on it. Why does nobody remove that? Does anybody complain? Nobody complains these days. Our telly's had a buzzing noise for the past three weeks. Will my dad complain? Will he fuck. Next door's weeds are growing in our garden. Will my dad complain? Will he fuck.

Ah, the town centre. Is that Dostoyevsky? Is there anything
in the town centre worth looking at? A woman pushing a
fully loaded shopping trolley out of a public toilet and a
hippy carrying half a loaf. Pretty interesting, I suppose.
You are what politicians call the vast majority of ordinary
people, you know that? You'd be amazed at some of the shit
you're in favour of.

'Hey, pal, could you buy us some glue?'

WHAT!

'Could you buy us some glue, please?'

A skinhead saying please, wow. Nah, you should try the
mushies. They're free. Ha ha. God, I'm cool. 'Eh. No, sorry.'
God, I sound a right prick when I speak. Is he following
me? No. Thank fuck for that. How come those guys look
so tough? Do they do training or what? Maybe it's just
the haircut. Nah, they've got more muscles than I'll ever
have. They've led hard lives. Every gesture they've made
was training. I've led a very sheltered life. Terasa told me
that. That's what she thinks about me. Pretty accurate
assessment actually. She also said I was a selfish bastard.
I don't like thinking about that. Should I go into the
bookie's and see if Mental's there. Nah, I've never been in
a bookie's in my life. Stop playing the detective, will you.
If you bump into people, you bump into them. You can't
force these things, can you? He won't be in the bookie's
anyway. Positive defeatism, that's me. There's that woman
from down the road that fancies me, oh yes she does.
Look at her. Oh no, she's going to say hello to me . . .
how come she never said hello. God, I nearly did. I'm
blushing. I know it. I'm blushing. Oh God, I'm going
to kill myself. Ah, the library. Wonder if there are any
gorgeous women in here. Mind her that came in here all
the time? God, she was sexy. She was wonderful. I'll have a
look through the recently returneds: John Buchan, Catherine
Cookson, Italo Calvino, Arthur Hailey, Frank O'Connor.
All these old women like their reading. Computers, chess,
biographies, economics, upper body development. This is
what we want. Yes, Daley, I'm sure you achieved that
physique by doing these poxy wee exercises. Mmmmmmm,
that looks interesting. I think you're best to use weights.

94

Maybe I should go down to the complex and use theirs. I don't want to become one of those fat bastards, though: fat neck, fat arms, fat legs. Ugh.

'Hello, Archie. Didn't know you could read.'

WHAT!!

'Oh. Hello, Robert. Just looking at the pictures. What you doing in here?'

'I'm spraying my car. I was just in seeing if they've got any books with any tips, you know.'

Why do you always scuff your feet on the floor when you talk? Stand still when you talk to me! I'm going to stagger you, Robert. Listen to this: 'I believe it's important to make sure you keep the can at a constant distance from the car.'

'Yeah, that's right. You working?'

'No. Too shy.' GOD BLESS YOU, STEVEN PATRICK MORRISSEY!

'There's talk of them laying off folk down at our place, some of the day workers. I think we're safe, though. Touch wood.'

'You should come on the dole, play football with us.' You've got that massive willy, I recall. Down to your knees. Great big greasy ugly thing it is.

'I'd love to play five-a-side again. They were great times. I go out jogging twice a week. I've done two half-marathons this year. What's this, anyway? You becoming a Big Arnie?'

'No, Marvin Hagler. No, I just wanted to see about broadening my shoulders and chest.'

'You have got quite a narrow chest, Archie.'

WHAT!

'Anyway, Archie, I'll need to get going. Keep in touch, okay?'

'Right. Cheerio, Robert.'

What the fuck do you mean, 'Keep in touch'? Am I out of touch or something. I bump into you about twice a year. You talk about cars and work. Oh God, I never asked for his wife. Ohhhhhhhh. I should've. We grown-ups do that sort of thing. I bet I freaked him out with my car spraying knowledge. You'd be amazed at some of the useless shit I've accumulated over the years. Am I 'out of touch'? I suppose so. I've led a very sheltered life. I'm bored in here. Let's go round to Casino Boogie and raid the cheap singles box.

There's always some new ones on a Thursday. I'll come back
to the library next week and join the record library. I'll
have finished *The Iron Staircase* by then. 'Doodoo doodoo
doodoo doodoo doodoo doodoo doodoo!' I will not look
at any of these dogs. I will not. I see you've still got your
'Victory to the Miners' sticker on the door. Is that going
to stay there forever? Right, a look through the new LPs
first. Try and look interested. Mmmmmmmmmm. Now the
cheap singles. Shit. Shit. Shit. Shit. *Slippery People!* Magic,
I'm having that. Brilliant. Anything else. *Lady Marmalade.*
Unbelievable. What a day! This is great. I'm blushing again.
   'A pound, please.'
   'Right, thanks.'
   I'll have a look through the T-shirts. See if there's any-
thing cheap and obscure. No, never is. I always wait for the
great T-shirt and twelve-inch sale. I mean nobody buys any
of these T-shirts and nobody buys twelve-inch singles. Well,
I don't. *Slippery People* and *Lady Marmalade*, for a quid.
Who's the greatest record blagger in the world, eh? Now
let's see, slip-pery peop-le. Even. Magic. Lady Marmalade. Odd. Shite. The Staple Sing-ers. Magic. Lab-elle. Odd.
But when you join title and artist they're both even. Magic.
Why did I start all this shit? Every phrase has got to be
even or odd. And I always want even to win. God knows
why. I'm odd. Blue-and-yellow's odd (but even when you
add the middle names — and I think you should). God's
odd. I suppose I have to have everything nice and tidy even.
Is that Dostoyevsky? No. He's odd. Marvin Hagler's even.
Prince. Prince Edward. The Undertones are odd. John Peel's
even but John Ravenscroft's odd. Oh Archie, how come you
never get bored? You're ugly, you should do. There's one
of those door-to-door religious shits that drag young kids
around and smile like perverts. God, you are frightening,
madam. Do you believe all that shit? Mind that time I had
an argument with one of them at the doorstep. Heh heh. My
mum came rushing out shouting 'Don't you corrupt my son.'
There's the massively endowed Robert again. I'll nip into the
job centre to avoid him. Ah, let's see if there's anything for
a nervous punk. Surprisingly few opportunities in that area
actually. God, you see some right drongoes in here. See that

guy wearing a tie; he's got two labelled carrier bags, he's studying training applications for which he's too old and he's whistling. I bet you can still belt out *My Way*, eh? No regrets in your life ... sorry, I'm being unfair. This place gives me the creeps. I'm off. Oh God, there's Syme. Look at his fucking muscles. Look at his face, though. If ever a face needed a visit to Lourdes. Shite, he's going to talk to me. Fake indifference. God, I need the toilet. Every part of my body needs the toilet. What is he going to say?

'See that cunt pal you got? Says he's wanting off our wagon. That's not on. Fucking shite. He can't do that.'

Twelve

Syme had GRFC tattooed on his knuckles and UVF on his neck. Archie felt uncomfortable, as though he were wearing somebody else's underpants — somebody else's dirty underpants.

'What you talking about?' asked Archie with faked indifference.

'Fuck off.' Syme walked away. His feet said the time was ten to two and he couldn't walk a straight line. He always walked like that.

Archie felt a rush of blood. What was going on? He walked back through the town and headed down the High Street. The town was filling with schoolchildren and people finishing work.

'Hey,' said Mental smiling like a brand new dad. 'Guess what? I've just done my annual shoplift. Absolute classic. Went up to Boots and nicked a record cleaning cloth. Easy as hell.' Mental was accompanied by Wee Stevie.

'I've just bumped into Syme. He was saying something about Davie shifting his job, to get away from Syme, like.'

'What was he saying?' asked Mental.

'That's what he said.' Archie didn't mention the tone.

'Fuck,' said Wee Stevie. 'I'd rather work with plutonium

than Syme. He's a bastard fuck. Everybody knows that. He shouldn't expect folk to dig him.' Wee Stevie was indifferent, nothing bothered him. 'I'm getting a jaunt down to Live Aid together, you digging it?' Wee Stevie asked Archie.

'I suppose so,' said Archie. He turned to Mental. 'You going?'

'If everyone else is.'

'Magic,' said Wee Stevie. 'We'll have enough for a coach, no problem fuck.' Wee Stevie was a small-town promoter, manager, supporters club secretary and drug-dealer. Always smalltown. Richard said he was devious, that he told lies and betrayed trust. Archie didn't like him because he let the-guy-that-never-talks-to-us and Chas and Rab decorate a wall of his flat with racist graffiti. 'Just a joke fuck. We're the least racist people you could ever hope to meet,' Stevie had said. Maybe. Wee Stevie at times resembled Elton John in his refusal to be anything other than apolitical. Of course he was anti-apartheid, he just wasn't paranoid by it fuck.

'I'll give you a phone after tea,' said Mental. 'We're going back to Stevie's, he's got a couple of my records.'

'I'll see you later,' said Archie.

'See you,' said Stevie.

Archie headed back to the shopping precinct. He was glad he had bumped into Mental. Meeting Syme had disturbed him, frightened him even. Syme was like the skinheads, tough, and he'd never forgiven Archie for altering the shape of his nose. Archie was disappointed Mental hadn't shown more concern. Probably because Wee Stevie was there.

'Steak pie, roast lamb, sausages.' Archie addressed Dostoyevsky.

The dog had just done a crap. He looked at it shamefaced. *Look at it. That ain't dogshit, that's horseshit — the shit of a horse! They fucking laugh at me, you know.*

Archie could see Richard in Casino Boogie with the owner, Ken Wilson. Archie refrained from entering. He didn't want to invade their conversation, their friendship. So he sat down, lit a cigarette and surveyed the shopping precinct.

The chain stores were located in the precinct: *Boots, Frozen Food, 'Woolies', Job Centre.* The family businesses remained in the High Street. Archie felt sorry for an old woman carrying a shopping bag. Her skin was white and her stride was infinitesimal. She looked round as if she was looking for somebody. Her glasses were as thick as the bottom of a milk bottle. Archie recalled seeing a similarly old woman walking across a piece of wasteground. Archie stopped the woman and asked her what she was doing. She said that she was taking a short-cut, that it was a lovely day, that her home help was on holiday, that she was expecting visitors at four and that she was ninety-five. Archie took the woman's bags and escorted her home. She blethered all the way, oblivious to Archie's interruptions. When Archie left she was preparing tea for her visitors at four. The neighbours frowned at Archie as he left the old woman's house as if he had done something wrong.

Three leather-jacketed, spiked-topped punks approached Archie.

'You got 10p?' one of them said.

'What?'

'10p. We've got no money.'

'No,' said Archie. This was too much. The punks walked away. Archie shook his head and said, 'Dearie dear.'

Eleven trees lined the centre of the precinct. Four secured bicycles and three secured dogs. Rogue shopping trolleys lay about, metal tumbleweeds. The town was only busy on Fridays and Saturdays.

The noise from the bookie's tannoy droned on. Loud enough to be an irritant. Archie sucked on his cigarette. The tannoy was incessant. On the previous Saturday's *Grandstand* Frank Bruno was asked where his money would be going on the Hagler fight. Big Frank said the best place for your money was your pocket and that Hagler would win. A million bookies cried. Archie wondered what he would tell Richard about Syme. Make a joke of it, he decided.

Richard emerged from Casino Boogie. He was wearing a yellow T-shirt, a black dress jacket, bleached Levi's and his black gutties.

'Hello. I was told you bought *Slippery People* and *Lady Marmalade*.'

'Yeah. Not bad for a pound.' Archie was surprised he'd been talked about. What else did they say?

'I was in seeing about an REM bootleg, one with forty cover versions,' said Richard.

'That should be great.'

'Hey, there's the Kid.'

The Kid was carrying a couple of LPs.

'Here comes the thief,' said Archie.

'What?'

'I did my annual shoplift the day. It was so easy. A record cleaning cloth out of *Boots*.' Mental smiled like a really cool bastard.

'Is it worth it?' said Richard. 'What if you'd got caught? Fancy going to court?'

'No court. I got away. Obviously, I wouldn't have done it if I was going to get caught. Wee Stevie's organising a trip down to Live Aid, you digging it?'

'Do any of his schemes ever come off?'

'Well, we won't get to go if we don't try.'

'I suppose so. Just for the cause though. I refuse to enjoy Dire Straits or whoever.'

'Same here,' said Mental. 'I'm going 'cause it's history in the making. I'm not going for a piss-up. I'm not even taking drink. Won't be able to afford it anyway.' Mental was dressed as he had been the previous evening.

'What records did you loan Wee Stevie?' asked Archie.

'*A Wizard, A True Star* and *Dixie Chicken*.'

'And what else was he saying, apart from "fuck"?' enquired Richard.

'Eh, nothing much. Could you give us 10p so as I can phone Davie. It's just that Archie was talking to Syme earlier and apparently there's been some shit going down.'

'Sure.' Richard sought out some change while Mental related what Archie had told him earlier. Archie was glad Mental was showing some concern. He'd watched them grow up, Mental and Davie: Celtic and Rangers, Marlboro and Regal, Guinness and Heavy. Only when Mental went round to see Terasa with a bottle of wine had they really fallen out. During the 'cold war' that followed they continued to play football but never talked to each other. One day an argument started about whether the Rangers team that won two trebles was any good. Mental challenged anybody present to list the Rangers team of that time. If they were any good, then the players would be easy enough to remember, he reasoned. Only seven names were mentioned and Mental thought he'd won his argument. Davie proceeded to name the thirteen players he considered to be integral in those seasons. Mental was furious at being wrong and said that they were crap anyway. As a consequence, Davie and Mental started talking, well arguing, again.

Mental phoned using one of the call boxes at the Post Office.

'What's up?' he asked as Davie answered.

'Nothing. Nothing's up.' Davie sounded subdued.

'Syme was talking to Archie . . .'

'What was he saying?'

'Said you'd asked to be put on a different wagon.'

'So.'

'"So", is that all you've got to say? Nothing else.'

'No.'

'Still going down the pub tonight?'

'Any reason why I shouldn't be?'

'I'll see you there then.'

'See you later. Cheerio.'

'There's been an argument there,' said Mental as he replaced the receiver. 'Terasa's got one hell of a temper. She says he never sticks up for himself, that he never complains about anything. That's true. He's soft as piss. He doesn't complain. He'd never take back a scratched record in his life.' Mental puffed. 'He can't take a slagging, though, even *I've* got to be careful what I say.'

'If he's getting picked on at his work, it can't be very pleasant for him,' said Richard.

'That's the thing,' agreed Mental. 'It's bad for him not to moan, so when he does it makes you wonder what the fuck's going on. Something must've really upset him.'

Archie refrained from playing the detective. He didn't want to discuss Davie. It was like discussing illnesses after a funeral — but that's what people discussed after a funeral. He tried to change the conversation. 'Who's all going to Live

Aid, anyway?'

'Eh,' said The Kid, preparing to count his fingers. 'There's Wee Stevie and Sonia and the-guy-that-never-talks-to-us; Stevie's wee sister and two of her pals; Ken Wilson and his wife; Senga Somerville and her new bloke Tony — that guy with the Kawasaki 750, do you know him?' Richard shook his head. 'He's a great lad, Hendrix fanatic, hates Heavy Metal, though — and Chas and Rab'll be going and myself and Archie. There's a lot of possibles. Stevie's coming down the pub tonight to see if we can get more names.'

'And how is he going to get tickets?' Richard sounded sceptical.

'If anybody can, he can.' Mental smiled with admiration.

'He's a devious bastard,' said Richard. 'If it requires lying and cheating, he should get them all right. Was he wearing those trousers? The ones he claims to have bought for fifty pence at a jumble sale and Kelly seen him buying them for twenty-five quid in that boutique over the town.'

'No,' laughed Mental. 'He's looking really cool just now. Black shoes, black T-shirt, black trousers, black raincoat and his hair cropped. Stop slagging Stevie, anyway. He's my kind of hero: parties like hell but appreciates a good rose. He said that *A Wizard, A True Star* was the best non-punk LP of the seventies. There's nothing wrong in that.'

'He's just agreeing with you. He never does anything for himself. He's a leech.'

'Right.' Mental adopted a challenging tone. 'Want a bet? I bet he gets this Live Aid thing going.'

'Okay, if we go to Live Aid, you get to sleep with my dog; if we don't go, my dog gets to sleep with you.'

'Fuck off.'

Fuck off!

They walked homeward. Dostoyevsky bounded like a police dog. He sensed tension in the air. For the first time in ages he didn't feel hungry, he felt high.

Richard and Mental continued to debate the merits of Wee Stevie. It all revolved around the word 'devious'. Stevie was Mental's Friday night let's-get-wrecked-and-chase-women buddy. Drugs and women were his specialist subjects for *Mastermind*. A fortnight previous he had tried to organise an attempt at the world record for non-stop snooker playing. It never materialised. It always seemed as if other people let him down, as if they were to blame. When he turned up at people's homes at half eleven at night, stoned out of his brain, most people took him in and gave him tea and sympathy. Richard, though, almost set Dostoyevsky on him. Trouble was Stevie needed to air his self-pity in public. He could never cut himself off like Richard. He needed people every minute of the day.

'You see the thing is,' said Richard, 'he is always in debt. He's never solvent. And he has the gall to go up to other people to ask them for money ... and he gets it! You can see he's got a permanent smirk on his face. *Devious.* What does he do with his money, anyway? He doesn't buy records, his mam buys all his clothes for him, he goes round there for all his meals and you'll never see him buy a round of drinks.'

'He puts 10p in a swear box every time he says "fuck",' suggested Archie.

'It's amazing he still does that,' said Mental. 'That's why he's so cool. He never changes, he's got style. He's like George Melly. He's got a specific way of talking. He's even got a specific way of walking. You know, that dead slow stagger.' Mental imitated the walk. 'Like a drunk poof.'

'He owes Senga Somerville forty quid,' said Richard. 'He's avoiding her. You'll notice he always looks over his shoulder, that's why.'

'Mind that time he borrowed her leather jacket for two months,' said Archie.

'I know,' giggled Mental, 'she beat the shit out of him. He borrowed her jacket to go to Edinburgh for the day and never came back for two months. Absolute classic.'

Senga Somerville had the best leather jacket in the world. Her leather trousers were pretty neat too. She and Richard bought the only two copies of *Anarchy in the UK* that reached town. There was a strong rumour that she had slept with Paul Simenon of The Clash. She said that Richard was a good guy because he bought a lot of reggae and she'd beaten up The Mental Kid after he'd started a rumour that he'd slept with her. Archie had never really had any dealings with her.

'Right then, Archie, you popping round for *Top of the Pops?*' said Richard.

'Will do.'

'Okay, see you later. See you Mental.'

Mental and Archie walked down the road. Mental looked back over his shoulder and put his hand atop his mouth. 'See when my big sister used to go out with him, she said he was so fucking intimidating. He's got such a chip on his shoulder. I don't like him slagging off Stevie.' Mental was agitated. 'I don't like it at all. It's none of his business what Stevie does with his money.'

'Come on, Wee Stevie gets a few folks' backs up. I can't stand him much. He still owes me a fiver.'

'What? You never said.'

'It was when we were at school.'

'Oh, for fuck's sake, Archie. You're so *naive.*'

'I'm just joking. but I'm sure he remembers the loan and I'm sure there's a part of him feels very smug that he got away without paying it back, know what I mean?'

'I'll say it again. You're so naive, Archie.'

Archie felt comfortable walking with The Kid. When he talked it was like thinking aloud. Mental started talking about football. Archie was pleased there was no further talk of Syme and Davie. What could they have said anyway? It was like liberals, Tories, parents and Wee Stevie said; don't think about things that upset you. Don't talk about apartheid, racism, sectarianism, slavery, starvation, injustice, corruption, exploitation, deception, torture, brutality and all those things. Gossip instead: football, Wogan, dish the dirt on friends and take the piss out the fat guy: Archie felt good talking about football, it was therapeutic. But a great big rumble in his stomach reminded him he was in dire need of a crap.

'I'll see you down the pub then,' said Mental.

'You okay for money?'

'Yeah. My sister's going to buy me a drink tonight. I've got enough to party with Stevie tomorrow and then the football on Saturday and that's it till my next giro. I'm not going out Saturday night.'

'Okay,' said Archie. 'Be good.'

Thirteen

Archie felt good. He decided to run home, not jog. It was five-fifteen and he was late for his tea. His legs and arms felt heavy; sore at the insides of the elbows and the backs of the knees. But it was a good pain. He didn't feel hungry but he didn't feel ill. The sweat ran down his ribs and he ran faster.

'She fancies you!' The shout came from a group of schoolgirls.

'I do not,' said the tallest one as she pushed the tell-tale-tit into the road.

Archie smiled and stopped running. The tall girl was blushing. So was Archie. Being fancied by extremely tall eleven-year-olds wasn't that bad, he decided. He smiled and waved at the girls.

As he expected, his mother and father had had their tea. There were potatoes, stewed steak and cabbage in the big pot. He turned the ring to two-and-a-half. The teapot was still hot enough. Archie went to the toilet and joyously emptied his bowels.

'I'm home,' Archie announced his arrival in the living-room. 'Sorry I'm late, I got delayed.'

'Isabel was just off the phone,' said Archie's mother. 'My Uncle George passed away last night.'

'I'm damned if I know where it is,' said Archie's dad. 'Remember, he was standing by Sheila's car — the old Austin — with his elbow on the roof.'

The shoeboxes of black and white photographs were out. The newspaper was unopened and the television was dormant. At his grandfather's funeral, Archie cried while his relatives wished each other a Happy New Year. It made him angry. Uncle Paul wished Archie a Happy New Year and Archie told him to fuck off. Archie stormed out and went straight home, missing the burial. Archie continued to show his disdain for the family by refusing to shake hands or acknowledge the New Year. It was a puerile gesture but it made him feel good. He often questioned whether it was right to be offended by such harmless people. He decided it was.

'I'll need to watch my stew.' Archie returned to the kitchen and stirred the food into a gooey muck.

They'll not get their visit, thought Archie. They'll get a funeral, though. Dad'll have to see about getting off work, mum'll have to see about ordering a wreath. There are too many deaths in this family. What's it going to be like growing old and hearing of the deaths of people I went to school with? Please God, no!

'The Funeral Groupies' was what Archie called his greater family. There was Uncle Bob who averaged a funeral a week. His record was three in a day; four over a twenty-four-hour period. He went to funerals where he didn't know the deceased or any of the close family. Auntie Liz was an expert on funeral convention. If the right people didn't get the cords she did not hide her disapproval. And as for those who didn't turn up and pay their respects . . . Conversation was restricted to hospitals and funerals. They knew which hospitals had the best reputation and which had the highest fatality rate. They retold stories of drunken ministers, undertakers that demanded to be paid after the burial and motorcades that got lost. Euphemisms were always used for death; 'polished off' and 'blew his fuse' by the men and 'passed on' by the women. When receptions were held the drinks were expected to be laid on. All these people had no weddings to look forward to. The only family get-togethers were funerals. Archie was the only one of marriageable age and they'd given up hope on him. Uncle Paul was the family guru. His politics and morality stood for the family. As a child, Archie loved him dearly. Now, Archie considered him a pervert. Archie had laughed at Uncle Paul looking through the pages of catalogues studying the women's underwear section and saying 'Oh, gosh . . . my goodness'. Page after page, he studied every kind and colour of garment. Once Uncle Paul undressed in front of Archie. The ugly penis hanging below the string vest was a picture that would stay with Archie forever. During an argument over Uncle Paul's influence on the family, Archie told his father of the incident. His father made light of it, saying that they were all country folk and nobody bothered about these things. But, Archie said, that memory had been imposed on him; you shouldn't do things that are going to cause unpleasant memories for children. Archie's father, though, sided with Uncle Paul. Maybe Archie was wrong to hate his family so much, they were just eccentric. Richard said it was the interbreeding that caused so many mongols in the country — the Tory stronghold. Archie laughed but it was his worst nightmare that Uncle Paul was really his father.

Archie ate his tea with relish. He was in a funny mood. Thoughts of his relatives always made him angry but he also felt nervous. Strange. He washed the dishes and wiped the table, sink and draining board.

That's your dinner you've had it. That was what his mother always said. Ever since he'd been a baby.

The phone rang. It was Roger Watson, a member of the family but not a blood relation. He wanted details of the funeral. Archie handed the phone to his dad. Business.

Roger Watson called black people 'darkies' and once gave Archie a half-hour lecture on how the Irish boil potatoes. He knew everybody's address, birthday and age — the family archivist. He claimed to be able to tell the difference between fifty brands of whisky by taste alone. A bachelor with a small farm outside Glasgow, his worldview was singular and quixotic. Archie thought he was a weird bastard. His eyebrows were as one and he carried a ghetto-blaster in his tractor playing Scottish dance music all day.

The bedroom was chilly. Archie had left the window open. He said 'Shit' and shut it. He removed his records from their paper bag and put the paper bag into a polythene bag that served as a bucket. He looked at the records with pride.

Lady Marmalade first. Awesome. He played it again. Even better. He recalled a picture of the girls in space-age costume: Nona Hendryx in a white body-stocking; Patti Labelle looking old and motherly, like Winnie Mandela, and a bit silly; and the other one with the silver bra. 'Voulez-vous couchez avec moi.' Archie assumed it was dirty. It was embarrassing to be told what records were about; to be told that rock 'n' roll meant fucking and what Johnny Bristol was on about when he sang 'Hang on in there, baby'. It was a bit sad in a way. John Peel once said that the only lyric that he understood was The Jam's version of the *Batman* theme. After the third play Archie took the record off and looked at the label. Another great record produced by Allen Toussaint. Archie resolved to find out more about Allen Toussaint. The B-side, *Space Children*, was written by Nona and it was awful.

Archie played *Slippery People* four times in a row. It was even better than *Lady Marmalade*. He imagined old Pop Staples and the girls dancing in unison for the verses then going daft during the chorus. The B-side was a boring ballad. He would play neither B-side again. Archie's record collection had mushroomed over the past few years. He knew he would be buying records for the rest of his life. And if he ever started to sit down and listen to them he wanted to be shot.

Six-thirty. Archie lit a cigarette and turned on the radio to get the news. The smell and taste of the cigarette were great. This was a good smoke, best for ages. Archie could imagine the eyebrows of the newsreader being raised and the smile being released for the silly story at the end. In olden days, newsreaders were required to dress in accordance with the dignity of the job. The contemporary newsreader had to be compatible with the personality of the job.

After the news, a Joni Mitchell track was played. Archie looked at one of his pictures of Marvin Hagler. There was no footballer's pose, no athlete's zeal, no rugby lad's worldliness or tennis player's pose. Hagler looked like the first few seconds of Jimi Hendrix's *Purple Haze* come to life.

Joni Mitchell ceased singing and Archie failed to catch the name of the track. He wasn't sure whether he liked Joni Mitchell. Another artist to check out at the record library.

The phone rang. It was Mental.

'I phoned up Davie again. Everything's calmed down. The guy from his work phoned him up to say he wasn't going to be working with Syme.'

'That's good,' said Archie, although he was unsure why he said that.

'Kelly and Louise are going down the pub tonight. So I'll go with them.'

'You still chasing Louise?'

'I don't chase women, they chase me. I play it cool.' Mental sounded cool.

'I'm going round for Richard shortly so I'll see you later.'

'Yeah.' Mental hesitated for a few seconds and then added, 'And be good.'

'Okay,' said Archie. Mental had never said 'be good' before — Archie said it all the time. Sometimes he forgot how shy The Kid was. It was nice to be reminded. Archie felt his eyes glisten as he wanted to giggle.

Archie felt so good he took out the headphones and listened to *Slippery People* and *Lady Marmalade* at ear-shattering volume. He danced about his room, knees and elbows in motion. Fuck Joni Mitchell, this was the stuff.

After a good wash, Archie put on his slip-ons and was ready to go. No Simenon tonight. He still felt nervous. In the hall Archie could hear his parents laughing at the TV. Archie was never sure whether they conversed while the TV was on. He hoped they said more than, 'That's him that used to be in *Z-Cars* . . . She was in *Crossroads*.' Once Archie had an argument with his father about the amount of television the latter watched. This was when his father said, 'Don't lecture me, you haven't earned the right'. Archie's father had always been relaxed and affable; increasingly he was sullen and apathetic. Mr Easy-Going meet Mr Couldn't-Give-A-Shit. He said 'I'm not bothered' an awful lot. He said 'Cheers' whenever he talked to Archie's friends on the phone. Archie considered it a forced affability. The happy-go-lucky approach seemed a bit desperate these days.

Archie checked his cash (four pounds, enough), cigarettes (need more, shit), matches (likewise) and watch. He decided he wanted to hear more records so he sought out Big Youth's *Ten Against One,* The B52's *Give Me Back My Man* and Buster Brown's *Sweet 94.* Archie recalled buying the records: the first one 10p at Oxfam, bargain of the century, easily; the second-named he bought at the time of its release; the Buster Brown single was one of twelve Charley R&B EPs he bought at Casino Boogie when the lot were sold for 50p each. Archie listened to the records while staring out the window. His head nodding in accompaniment. It was one of those nights when he would have been quite happy to stay in listening to records.

When the records were finished Archie went through and checked his appearance in his parents' mirror. When he had started High School, all the hard men had acknowledged his presence with a nod. Did he look hard? He didn't know. Not pretty, not handsome, nor fat nor big nor small. Archie took a deep breath. He decided against wearing a jacket. It would be cold but he didn't want to wear one.

'I'm away then. Did you find the photograph?'

His mother pointed to the mantelpiece. On it there was a photograph of a man standing beside a car. 'It was in with your father's National Service pictures,' she said. She was reading the local freesheet.

'Well, I don't know how the blazes it got there,' said Archie's father.

'Did you see the fight?' asked Archie.

'Yeah. Some fight, eh?'

'Great. I'm away for Richard.'

'Cheerio, son,' said Archie's mum. She increasingly called him 'son'. She fixed Archie with the same look she had used earlier. Archie shivered. I am the most important person in their lives, he told himself.

It was freezing outside. Archie went to the mini-market and bought cigarettes and matches. The girl smiled and made a comment about the weather. Archie was pleased. Mental said that the Asian community never smiled or spoke. Archie could tell him he was wrong.

The problem was to fit the extra cigarettes and matches into his pockets. Why did I not just leave the other packet at home?

Archie went the back way to Richard's to avoid passing Mental's flat. It would mean getting his shoes mucky but he always felt uncomfortable walking past without going in. It seemed . . . wrong.

'Man on! Man on!' A group of young boys were playing football at the back of the garages. 'You're a fucking arse-hole, Watson, you know that,' screamed one of them. The ball went flying in Archie's direction. The shot would have hit the corner flag on a full-size pitch.

Archie went out of his way to retrieve the ball. He attempted the world record for keepie-uppie. He managed three.

'What a fucking tube,' said Watson.

'It's Michel fucking Platini,' said the one who had shouted at Watson.

Archie tried again. He managed six. He tried again. Two. The young footballers applauded. Archie smiled and fired a shot at the one who had compared him with Michel fucking Platini. The ferocity of the shot impressed everyone, including Archie.

'That's not Platini, that's Davie Cooper,' said the one who had shouted at Watson. A Hun.

'Garbage,' said Watson. 'More like Davie Provan, the best dead ball expert in the world.'

Archie smiled and let them squabble. Later on they would meet up with the girls at the adventure playground. They would talk and tease and get bored. How could you get bored with football and girls? But Archie knew that when he was their age he did.

When the council introduced free sports facilities for the unemployed, Archie played indoor football twice a week. After a while, though, Archie got frustrated. He was a bad loser. Mental and Davie would have played every day. Mental ran till he was throwing up blood and was not averse to blessing himself and screaming 'And he makes the tea as well' after scoring a goal.

On the way to Richard's, Archie encountered three young couples looking happy and lovely, and a group of young cyclists organising a ten-lap Tour de Logie Baird Drive. In an enclosed drying green Archie could see Paddy with his two pals. Charlie Nicholas had a carrier bag. The bag drooped as though it had something heavy in it. Stop playing the detective, Archie told himself. It's none of your business. Have you ever seen Paddy outdoors at night before? No, never. There you go, you shouldn't be shocked then. People appear suspicious when you encounter them out of context, like bumping into your dad over the town. Or the Queen in *Low's*.

The glass had been cleared away from the entrance to Richard's close. The tenants had given their decision on the new entryphone system and ripped it out of the wall.

Fourteen

'Fancy a cup of tea?' asked Richard. The record being played was The Detroit Spinners' *Ghetto Child*.

'Sure,' said Archie. Richard went through to the kitchen. Archie looked at Dostoyevsky and said, 'What did you have for your tea?'

Brussels sprouts, nuts and boiled cabbage.

'Do you know what I would do if you attacked me?'

This should be interesting. Come on, I could do with a good laugh.

'Well, I could ram my arm down your throat, make you choke: I could put both my hands in your mouth like so, one-up one-down — jaw snaps; I could do a similar thing with your front legs, separate and snap; I could batter you with any available object; kick in the balls maybe.' Archie sucked air and bit his lower lip. 'Or I could grab you by the back legs and smash your skull off the pavement. Interesting, eh?'

Who do you think you're talking to? A fucking poodle? You've got a strange mind, pal.

Richard returned with two mugs of sugarless, milkless tea. He turned the volume of the television up. The theme music to *Top of the Pops* was playing.

When there were good records in the charts, *Top of the Pops* could be the best programme in the world: the *Pretty Vacant* promo, Siouxsie's kicks on *Hong Kong Garden*, the great Madness videos, Alex Harvey's *Delilah*, New Order (crap but live), PIL's *Flowers of Romance* with Johnny handing his fiddle to a member of the audience. Archie remembered Bolan's grin and Slade's boots, The Stylistics singing on top of a building and Barry White's girlfriends. Archie and Richard wanted to love every episode of *Top of the Pops* as if it was the best. But only when John Peel presented it did they pay special attention. They knew that if they were fourteen, watching The Smiths with their parents, their armpits sweating and unable to breathe, it would be special. Like taking a girlfriend home.

'You getting on all right with your folks?' asked Richard.

'Yeah. Touch wood. I still hate a lot of the things they do. I'm increasingly of the opinion that I'm the one that's fucked-up. We've had no major arguments for a while.' Archie didn't mention the death of Uncle George and the looks his mother gave him, although he would later perhaps. He wanted to confide in Richard.

'My parents have been really good to me of late. I think they've realised I'm not the waster they always assumed I was. And, as you said, as you get older it's easier to accept that you're the one that's fucked-up.'

'They were really good to you when Susan left.'

'I know,' said Richard. 'It just seemed strange my dad being understanding. He's never been particularly hip. Last summer he bought a safari suit!' Richard laughed. 'He still calls CND Ban the Bomb. I think people are more at home with their own understanding and terminology. It's like guys of my generation still use the same words to describe sex and football as they did when they first discovered sex and football.'

'Kelly and Louise are coming down the pub tonight.'

'As long as Kelly doesn't do her usual and go out of her way to disagree with everything I say. Mind that last time with her anti-abortion rant? "They put them in a bucket. That's what you do with rubbish." She was out of order.' Richard shook his head. 'It's just because I've been to university and I read books. They've always got to turn a discussion into a confrontation.'

'You went mad that time she compared you with Robert Elms.'

'I know. She can certainly get my back up, I'll say that for her. Terasa too. She can make me feel like shit.'

'She said that you are an inverted racist.'

'I'm not. It's not like Kelly and Mental going on about the IRA as if it was the most important issue. There's a certain type of IRA supporter with the homely jumpers and the passing acquaintance with Irish culture and history. They've got nicer accents and wardrobes than the Unionists. The difference between Gerry Adams and Ian Paisley is as much aesthetic as ideological. I find it laughable sometimes.'

'You'd be more supportive of the IRA if Ireland was in Central America.'

'You can't compare the situations. Catholics in the north have certain rights. I do believe in a United Ireland, but I don't think it would have much effect on the day-to-day lifestyle of anyone in the north. Whereas in Central America and South Africa, basic legislative changes would drastically affect the day-to-day lives of most people. My latest idea to put pressure on the South African government is for everyone to change their names to Nelson Mandela.'

'That's stupid.' Archie shook his head. 'The only way to achieve anything in South Africa is through violence, not sanctions, not boycotts, not political pressure but violence.'

'See if they had a civil war, like in the Spanish Civil War, and people went and fought the fascists, like George Orwell and Edward Heath did in Spain, would you go?'

'Yeah.'

'So would I. But I don't think people would think I was going for the right reasons. I don't know. I can see myself going out there with a leather jacket with "This machine kills fascists" written on the back, and I can also see myself being killed. But I would definitely go. That belief is important to me. I'd be prepared to die.'

'Do you think many people would go?'

'I shouldn't think so. It's like Mental says about the lifelong Labour supporters welcoming a black neighbour.

Fine, that's okay. But two black neighbours, three . . .'

'By the way,' said Archie changing the subject, 'I preferred *Five Leaves Left* to *Greetings from LA*. They were both great, though. Some voice Buckley's got.'

'I don't generally like acoustic-based music but Nick Drake was special.'

'I read in the *NME* that Gabrielle Drake was his sister.'

'Yeah,' said Richard. 'You'd expect him to be an only child. But they never are. Morrissey probably has five sisters.'

Top of the Pops finished and Richard played a video of Marvin Gaye miming *Can I Get A Witness* on *Ready Steady Go*. He was wonderful; beautiful and cool. Archie and Richard couldn't stop smiling at each other. So brilliant it made you blush. The clip finished and The Beatles appeared frolicking about to *Strawberry Fields Forever*. Richard stopped the tape.

'Was Marvin Gaye an only child?' asked Archie.

'No. There's at least one brother. I think when you're an only child you're more appreciative than creative. You appreciate things like books and records more. I'd have loved brothers and sisters. I'm sure life would have been easier. No intellectual anxieties. See when you go to Mental's there's always activity. Like the telly can be on and nobody will be watching it. Same with friends, they've got millions of them. Everything seems laid on for them. But I wonder if it's better to be that way or just have a few really close friends. Take Wee Stevie, for example. When we were ranting the other day he listed off his best friends. It was amazing. With Stevie like, you imagine him to have millions of friends. But the top five were Mental, the-guy-that-never-talks-to-us, Sonia, you and me. I was shocked. I hate his guts!'

'Probably just wanted to cadge money off you. Remember everything he does has an underlying reason. He has to leave with a smirk on his face. What about Chas and Rab and all that lot?'

'He says he sees them a lot but he's not close to them. I'm like you, I wonder why he said that? You've got to remember that he suffers from classic wee brother syndrome.

All those dopeheads do. Those people are so selfish and unreliable.'

'The trouble with having only a few friends is that they're all you've got,' said Archie. 'Without you and Mental I'd be lost . . . I think. Even with Davie I don't feel close. I feel really inadequate.'

'You should become a teacher, Archie.'

'I hate those words — "you should". All the times in my life I've needed advice and encouragement, everybody kept quiet. And now all I get is these ridiculous suggestions.'

'I wouldn't mind being a teacher. Coach the football team, stage plays, get Valentines from stupid girls. Great stuff. I'm too much of a prick, though. Your average hoodlum would take no time in getting me sussed.'

'Stop feeling so sorry for yourself,' said Archie in a Terasa-style voice.

What you need is a good feed. Get some steaks and chops in.

'I think Davie should get married soon,' said Richard. 'He should stop pissing about. You and Mental should be giving him more encouragement. You're his best friends. It's a touch cruel to say it, but Terasa is better than he deserves. They are a real couple. They're not two post-relationship depressives comforting each other, like you see in the paper. You know, damn near everybody from this town has married somebody from a different town. It's true. It's always somebody local marrying somebody from Fauldhouse or Milton of Campsie, whatever. Any obscure little place.'

'See Greg Hughes has just got engaged to somebody from Northern Ireland.'

'It's amazing.' Richard was smiling. 'It really is.' Archie smiled. There was never any laughing or giggling with Richard. The last time Archie had been helpless with laughter (without the aid of drink or drugs) was the episode of *Auf Wiedersehen, Pet* where Oz said, 'They bombed me grannie'. He watched the programme with his mum and dad. The three of them cried with laughter.

'I suppose I'll end up marrying somebody from a different town,' mused Richard. 'I wonder where they'll come from. I mean I never go out of my way to meet anyone and yet I still expect to get married.'

'I expect I'll only leave the parental home to enter the marital one. I'm too lazy to do anything else. God knows how it's going to happen.'

'I'm being a wee bit cynical, though. I'm sure a lot of people marry because they love each other.' Richard stopped and thought for a second. 'I've been trying to act less cynical of late. There's a lot of people these days who think they're being intelligent when they're being cynical and dismissive. You see them on *Question Time* — all those people who use cancer as a metaphor. It's like watching the mentally retarded interrogating the Gestapo. You have an audience of well-meaning, but ill-informed lefties who come across as ignorant thugs. Your average lefty talks in sentences either two thousand words long or two grunts short. It's either Kinnock's waffle or Skinner's I'm-a-moron-and-proud-of-it dogma.'

'When you let the general public have their say, it's sad that they aren't really adding to the debate. They just trot out these easily remembered clichés.'

'Yeah, like on *Right to Reply*,' said Richard, 'most of the people are just moaning. There's no attempt to raise the level of the moan, to articulate the moan.'

'Are you going to record *Question Time* so we can watch it later?' asked Archie.

'Suppose so. See the great British public at moan.' Richard found a tape and set the timer. He walked over to the hi-fi and put on *The Best of Bobby Bland*.

'See the difference between a Bobby Bland ballad and one of those film soundtrack ballads . . .' said Richard, his fury inexpressible in language.

'Have you heard *Do Me, Baby* by Prince?'

'No.'

'That's my favourite ballad. It's on *Controversy*.'

'All those Lionel Ritchie type ballads are so sanitised. They're sexless and soulless syrup.'

'I still like *Without You*. It's the lyric. I will always believe the guy meant it. It reeks of the *Our Tune* syndrome, though. Those couples always come from different towns.'

'I know it's always Sylvia from Chorley and Paul from Weston-Super-Mare. And their life is summed up by a Snowy White record. Pathetic. *Without You* was the one that started it, though.' Richard pointed an accusatory finger. 'I retain a certain fondness for that one, I must admit. It's always the case that good original stuff leaves a dire legacy. Like Hendrix left Heavy Metal, Ian Curtis left the Goths, and Edwyn Collins left us with all those horrible Glasgow bands.' Richard blew deeply. 'Fancy another cup of tea?'

'Okay. When we leaving?'

'The back of nine. We've plenty of time.'

'You'll get slagged off for being mean again.'

'Is that what they think of me?' Richard was hurt. 'See when I hear what people think of me, I get really freaked. I truly hate the person that a lot of people think I am. You get the likes of Wee Stevie making all these assumptions about me; the records I'm supposed to listen to, the books I'm supposed to read, I get really angry.'

'Wee Stevie says you're incredibly cool; says you've got everybody sussed.'

'You know this, he doesn't even know that I'm shy, that I'm a bit pathetic about things. Wonder what made him say that, anyway?' Richard played the detective. 'And on the other hand you've got Kelly and Terasa who think I'm a suicidally miserable bastard. And everybody goes on about me being serious all the time. How can I be serious all the time when I spend four or five hours a day up here listening to Tapper Zukie and Little Johnny Taylor! People don't see my shyness. I used to think Susan understood me . . . and then she fucked off.' Richard laughed and went through to the kitchen.

Archie stood up and stretched himself. He walked over to the dining table and looked at the new *NME*. Archie would buy his tomorrow. There was also a copy of *The Face*, a couple of mail order lists and a couple of obscure fanzines. Archie spotted a piece of paper with Richard's handwriting on it. He picked it up,

THE SHIT/THE DIFFERENCES

serious/intense
petulant/passionate
new/issues
enthusiastic greeting
get away with it/apologise

man's gotta do/macho bullshit
violence/punishment
what you been up to?/ a more

ambivalence/apathy

Archie felt rotten looking at the bit of paper but he couldn't resist a smile. He hadn't a clue what it was about. Later on he knew he would be playing the detective.

Richard returned with two mugs. 'It's like there are a lot of things in my life that I deeply regret having said or done. Not because they were wrong but because people have based their opinions of me on those actions, solely on those actions. I get very upset when people hold things against me. As I said, I hate the person that a lot of people think I am.'

'Earlier on I was trying to figure out what people thought of me.'

'Who like?'

'Parents, neighbours, girls . . . Just people.' Archie was petrified that Richard was going to tell Archie what he thought of him. Please God, no!

'Mind that time we were in that café and I started lecturing a wee boy about the evils of eating meat?' Archie nodded. 'Well, that incident has been exaggerated out of all proportions. According to legend, I shouted at him and made the wee boy cry. It was only a joke. The lad enjoyed his burger and his mam had a good laugh.'

'It's what people believe you're capable of, I'm afraid. Your aloofness is intimidating, threatening.'

'I think this is what Wee Stevie has been putting out about me. He's been building up a picture of me as the neighbourhood weirdo. The potential axe-murderer. It's all bullshit. I'm up here listening to my records and I'm perfectly happy. Sometimes I wish I could just stay up here all the time. See when you own more records, you play more records. When I started listening to records I would play them over and over again. Now that I've got a semi-decent record collection, I have to play records for four hours a day to stay appreciative. I love it. If you extrapolate this there will come a time when I listen to records for about ten hours a day. I still play singles five times in a row when I buy them.'

'I played *Slippery People* and *Lady Marmalade* three times each,' said Archie. 'The thing that bugs me about listening to my records is that nobody ever sees me when I'm that happy, and if they did they wouldn't understand.'

'Exactly, that ties in with what I'm saying. I'm perfectly happy in this selfish little world I've created for myself. It is a means to an end, though. I do intend to have my own record shop one day. But at this moment, this is right. My life is a list of records with some thoughts and observations thrown in. It's different and that's what I want. But see if I get a letter from Susan tomorrow . . .'

'Being ideologically sound's important as well,' said Archie with a laugh. 'That cuts you off from most people.'

'I'm sure my ideology derives in part from when I was a wee boy and I wanted the Indians to beat the cowboys.'

'I'll be selfish for a second and say that since I'm more important than you, it's time to go to the pub.' Archie stood up as if he was preparing to leave.

'Okay,' Richard smiled and swapped the Bobby Bland LP for *Yearful of Sundays* by King Sporty. 'I'll just get myself together, I won't be long.'

Archie lit a cigarette. He knew Richard would be putting on make-up and some of that coconut-smelling stuff on his hair. It would be a couple of minutes before he was back. Archie resisted the temptation to look at the piece of paper again. He walked over to the unit and picked out *The Encyclopaedia of Black Music*. He read the entries on Allen Toussaint and Labelle. There was a picture of Labelle in which they looked much as Archie recalled. Nona looked a bit ridiculous. Archie had seen her on the *Midsummer Night's Tube* singing with Frankie and she looked a lot better then. If I were Prince Edward, Archie said to himself.

'Right, Dostoyevsky,' said Richard. 'Archie's more important than me and Archie says it's time to go.'

I could do with a walk. I'm not saying I'm going to shit like but you never know.

'I'll take you for a walk later. Okay?'

No. A mildly pathetic expression adorned the Dobermann's face. When the house was empty he fantasised about burglars; fat, juicy burglars. Maybe one with a weapon, a crowbar say. *Fair fight, fair fight.*

'That's a good record, that,' said Archie.

'I'm obsessed with mid-seventies reggae just now. It's funny, with most forms of music, I hate people who talk of golden eras and the like, but I don't buy any new reggae releases. It's more the old stuff I pick up at record fairs. Wonderful it is.'

'*Yearful of Sundays.* It's like being on the dole,' joked Archie.

'It's Mental that really hates Sundays, eh?'

'Loathes them. He wanders round on Sunday afternoons telling everybody how much he hates Sundays.'

'Well, dog. We're away,' said Richard. 'Any burglars just kill them. Don't eat them. Just kill them.'

Chance'd be a fine thing.

Fifteen

Twenty-four-hour industry provided the smell and the soundtrack to their walk down the pub. There weren't many people going about. A few dog-walkers and bingo-goers, that was all. In the distance a youth could be heard shouting. The parent-hating, neighbour-baiting bravado fuelled by dare as much as devilment.

'Do you think that Davie's shown any signs of becoming a working-class caricature since he started work?' asked Archie. Richard hated caricatures: racial, social, class, psychoanalytical, sexual, sociopolitical, canine, astrological, whatever.

'He's got some disturbing symptoms: increased swearing and sick jokes, and his obsession with things fiscal. Work affects different people in different ways. It can be really intimidating. I've just finished a six-week stint at an Italian restaurant and when they ganged up against me it was pretty scary.'

'I think there's a difference between them and Syme.'

'It's the same thing.'

'Richard, you don't know people like that. You think that Chas and Rab are racist hard men. Syme makes them look like synchronised swimmers. You know when Chas tries to drink himself unconscious and he's got that look on his face, that stare, he looks completely deranged? Well, Syme is like that every minute of the day.'

'Sorry,' said Richard. 'I sometimes feel that the animosity that exists between Mental and Syme is a bit silly. They have never spoken to each other, remember.'

Between the physics and chemistry labs of the High School there was an alcove. The schoolchildren used it as a place to smoke, the adults used it as a public lavatory. More people had pissed there than at Heathrow Airport. An adult was using the alcove. He was fat, fortyish with a cheese and onion grin.

'There's that guy that looks like Ian McAskill,' said Archie.

'He does, eh,' agreed Richard. The bladder emptier bent his knees, straightened and turned round. He waved at Archie and Richard.

'Why do they always wave?' wondered Richard. 'I mean, do they expect us to wave back?'

'Aye, lads,' said the man. 'Rare night.'

'You okay?' asked Richard. The man added a laugh to his grin but said nothing. He staggered homeward. If he could've danced, he would've.

Richard said, 'They should do a *Forty Minutes* documentary on that alcove, the people that use it. Mental always pisses there, eh?'

'Yeah, I've seen him that desperate he's run to get there. I've seen him throwing up there. Can you see yourself at that age?'

Richard seldom spoke of ageing, he was private in that way. He spoke of his parents as people spoke of their neighbours.

'No. I live from day to day. I expect to die young, anyway. My lifestyle is geared towards being a really cool pensioner. By forty, I think I'll have gone. It's true. I should live to be ancient and get interviewed on the telly about my records and all the young punks would be saying, "Look at that old bastard. What a hero!" And I'd be raving on about the Pistols and whoever's The Mary Chain of the day. I'd slag off the fascists.'

They walked along at a fairly slow pace. Richard was the slow walker. He strolled, really. Archie wasn't that bothered. He did want to get to the pub, though, and see the others.

'I love walking,' said Archie. 'I used to walk for hours on Sunday mornings when I was a wee boy. Everybody else was at Sunday School. I used to walk over the park and have a round of putting then walk over the town. I loved getting soaked walking to school and then getting soaked walking home at dinner time. Magic.'

'Me and Susan used to go out walking at three o'clock in the morning. It was wonderful. I quite often take Dostoyevsky out at that time. He fair enjoys it. See this new cemetery they've got here, it really freaks me.'

'I know what you mean.'

The new cemetery was about the size of half a football pitch. It was bounded by trees on three sides and the main road on the other.

'You mentioned walking to school back there,' said Richard. 'I was always late for school. I was that busy listening to Noel Edmonds. I used to love him, thought he was great. I would meet up with John Williams and we would discuss all the silly phone calls and all that shit. I truly loathe Noel Edmonds now. I suppose it's a change of taste.'

'I thought you were the one that didn't believe in taste,' pointed out Archie.

'I've been thinking about this. There are certain factors which affect your appreciation and to simplify that notion, we use the word taste. For example, more people like Dire Straits than Captain Beefheart, but most people have never heard Captain Beefheart. So, question: would more people prefer the good Captain if they had heard him? Answer: no. Why? Because the factors which determine their appreciation dictate that they prefer Dire Straits. Different taste.'

'The word taste has a cultured ring to it, it shouldn't apply to Dire Straits fans.'

A car pulled up alongside Archie and Richard. A pretty girl leaned out the passenger seat and said, 'Excuse me, could you tell us how to get to Nevis Terrace, please?'

Richard squatted to the eye level of the girl as if he was going to be there for a while and said, 'No.'

'Simon Peters' place,' shouted the (not-so-pretty) male driver. 'He said it was near the traffic lights.'

'Oh,' said Richard. 'Right. Traffic lights. We've only got one set of traffic lights. That was clever. Eh, let me think. Go down to the end of this road and turn right at the junction. Then keep going till you reach the sports complex — it's a big building, you can't miss it — then first left after that and you should see the traffic lights in the distance.'

'Okay, I've got that,' said the driver and they were off.

'I'm really proud at having directed someone to a set of traffic lights,' said Richard. 'Normally I'm hopeless. I've lived here all my life and I haven't heard half the street names. I'm also told I don't have a local accent.'

'I asked my mum after somebody's been at me for directions,' said Archie. 'She always knows. It might take her half an hour to remember but she always gets there.'

'It's one of the hassles of being a pedestrian. I feel so rotten when I can't be of help. Once there was this lorry-driver and he was absolutely knackered — sweat dripping off him — and he wanted directions to the Bathgate road. The only way I could think of was through your estate. I never told him, though. There must be an easier road than that for a lorry. My mum and dad could tell you all the street names, who owns which shop, who used to own it, who built which estate; all the things I consider mundane. They know all about wiring and plumbing, and holidays and cars.'

'They don't know the important things like Howlin' Wolf's real name,' suggested Archie with a hint of sarcasm.

'That's different, that's interesting, that's my life. Plumbing isn't interesting. I was just thinking that at the High School just now there's a guy as much into my records as I am. A guy that can't wait for the next Smiths or REM LP. That's great. That's interesting. And I'm still like that. Plumbing isn't like that.'

'Some people would say you're as boring as they come.'

'I know. A white, Anglo-Saxon, Protestant, heterosexual, male, post-relationship depressive — pretty boring, I suppose. There are millions of us. But whereas they say "I'm not bothered", I always give a positive answer, even if it's "I don't know". See when we go down the pub tonight, there'll be a lot of indifference. I don't spend my time looking for such things, you just can't help but notice it.'

Archie decided to confide something that had been bothering him for the past twenty-four years. 'You know, I was born when the documentary started and ever since I've felt that there's been a camera following me, recording my every action. They decided to make a documentary on somebody's life and they selected me. I always feel as if everything I do, I'm going to have to justify it in the interview that's going to make up part two of the programme. This documentary, this life.'

Richard nodded sympathetically and said, 'Television has completely dominated our lives. Our memories are rectangular and we appear in them as if actors. We don't recall what we've seen, we recall what we were in. See when you see the bereaved on television, they must be acting, same with drug addicts.'

'What really bugs me is that I believe that everyone is in on this documentary . . . including you.'

'Look up the word solipsism in the dictionary. It may cheer you up, it may freak you out. But who wrote the dictionary?' Richard was being enigmatic.

They walked through the park and over the bridge. Archie stopped to light a cigarette. He asked Richard about Joni Mitchell and Allen Toussaint. Richard wasn't a Joni Mitchell fan. He said that the record library had a lot of her LPs and encouraged Archie to join. Richard hadn't known that Allen Toussaint had produced *Lady Marmalade*. He said that he had Dr John's *Gris Gris* album and that that had been produced by him. He offered to tape it for Archie.

'It's a great LP. Real rootsy,' he said. 'I'm really enjoying my records just now, all of them. Mental says that you can only appreciate music if you focus only on a particular style or aspect. I completely disagree with that. That's an excuse for embracing nostalgia. I played Elvis Presley's *Little Sister*, George McRae's *Rock Your Baby* and Barrington Levi's *Here I Come* before you came round and there is no way that I could have enjoyed those records more by adapting my circumstances. *Little Sister* didn't sound better thirty years ago and it wouldn't sound better if I was an Elvis nut.'

'Mental can get a bit sentimental about punk. He can tell you exactly where he was the first time he heard all the classic records.'

'And I believe he's telling the truth. He's like that. You can believe that he got carried away with it all. But as you said, sentimental, that's the word. That's what I think created punk. Sheer hatred of nostalgia. I remember in '76 there was this really gross Glenn Miller revival then K-pow, PUNK. Magic.'

'And all the old punks say "those were the days".'

'Only the arseholes, the hangers-on.'

The concentration of parked cars grew greater. They were nearing the pubs.

'You still go to the pictures a lot?' asked Archie.

'Yeah, every week. You should come up. Just a pound. It's nice and peaceful in the afternoons. You don't get all the kids in.'

'I slag my dad off for watching the telly in the afternoon. It would be a bit hypocritical.' When Archie went to the pictures, he couldn't help but imagine how bad his skin would look on the big screen.

'I like understanding good films. When I used to watch all the quiz shows and soap operas with Susan, I became an absolute boring bastard. I knew the capital of Tibet, I knew Henry the Eighth's third wife, I knew everything. And now I go round and see my mum and dad and they're watching *Blockbusters* and I just want to scream. The thing is that now that I've become a lot more catholic in my reading, I want to understand things where before I used to be an absorber of useless information.'

There were six pubs within a quarter mile of each other. They each catered for their own drinkers. The *Albany* catered for the young married males who wanted a game of pool and a rant about football and work. They had a wide range of beers and groups played there every Thursday. The barmaids were motherly and not averse to swearing. *Dingbats* was for the first-time drinkers. There were discos from Thursday to Sunday. People dressed in very dark or very light clothes. The Mental Kid held the record for being the youngest person served there — thirteen years and ten months. *Tropicana* was cavernous with a tiny bar and the draughtproofing of Stonehenge. Not very popular but the people who went there were regulars. The *Royal* was a hotel with a massive car park and it attracted people with cars. The barmaids wore uniforms of black skirts and white blouses while the male clientele had very large backsides. The *Gatsby* was where the post-relationship depressives went for company. There were always more women than men. And then there was the *Cabbage Patch*.

The *Cabbage Patch* attracted the sixth years, the students, the rugby club and the goths. It had the best seats and the biggest bar. It was always comfortably busy. Bob Johnson played records on Thursdays and Saturdays. He grudgingly played requests but played mostly the records he wanted to hear. The barmaids were always eighteen and looked like newsreaders' daughters.

'It's quarter to ten. Everybody should be here by now,' said Richard.

'You're like me, you've got a phobia about being the first to arrive.'

'This will be only the fourth time this year that I've been in a pub. I hate going into a pub by myself. That's one thing I can't fathom out about Wee Stevie. He can go into a pub and sit there on his own all night. He says he's the type of person that can do that.'

'There's Louise's car,' pointed out Archie.

'The inverted pram. Well, here we go. I always shite myself before I go into a pub. I wish this was *Cheers* where you walked through the door and everybody knew your name. I get a rush of blood when I walk through the door. I'm astonished I've never collapsed under the strain.'

'I hate it when you walk in and you think you recognise somebody out of the corner of your eye. But you're frightened to turn round and be really obvious or . . .'

'. . . or you find yourself eyeball-to-eyeball with some guy wielding an axe screaming "Who you looking at?" Yeah, I've done that a few times myself. What are you wanting to drink?'

'Pint of Carlsberg.'

'Okay. Here we go. God, I'm nervous. I bet Davie and Mental are talking about football.' Richard sighed. 'In the football game of life nobody passes the ball to me, you know that.'

They entered the pub.

Sixteen

There were about fifty people in the pub. Seven of them were male sixth-year students with blowdried hair and sports bags. They'd just arrived after playing indoor football. They were the sort of people you see driving about on a Sunday afternoon; five to a car. The goths were gathered round the machines. They never sat. Attired in studded noses, black clothes, matt black hair and big pointed shoes, the boys had long hair and the girls had short hair. Collectively, they wore thirty-eight bangles. Archie had always wanted to wear jewellery, not for the appearance but to rattle as you walk. He was fearful of the associations, though, and contented himself with picking the mud off his boots. Archie admired the goths. They were as musically unappreciative as the hippies and like the hippies they looked aloof. They varied their dress sense enough to refute allegations of uniformity.

There were three couples alone and two couples together. Couples who had initially spent every Sunday afternoon searching for somewhere to snog (empty school playgrounds, always the favourite) now sat looking as if they were waiting to be introduced. Richard said that sitting in a pub with a girl that you were in love with and saying nothing was wonderful.

Archie thought it looked boring and wanted to give them directions to the nearest school playground.

There were a few males sitting around in small groups of two or three having animated conversations. Archie recognised them but he didn't know them.

At the bar, there were two barmaids, a bar manager, nicknamed Hitler, and four resident bar-stool sitters, appreciative of the alcohol and the congenial atmosphere. Bob Johnson was playing the Ohio Players' *Love Rollercoaster*.

Bob Johnson had a strong claim to being the most wonderful man alive: Bob Johnson had 842 James Brown singles. Some found solace in love, some in religion, some in drugs and some in football. Bob, however, firmly believed that God had an Afro. Like Richard, Mental and Archie he gained a lot more pleasure from listening to records than he would have if he'd been involved in making them. During the day he worked on a 600-page biography of George Clinton and a discography on the history of funk. Like most people obsessed with music (save John Peel) he was exceptionally skinny. He was six foot and weighed nine and a half stone, fully clothed. His dress sense was limited to navy blue V-neck sweaters and jeans. BUT HE HAD 842 JAMES BROWN SINGLES!

Richard got the drinks in and he and Archie joined the others. They sat in the farthest corner. Louise, Kelly, Terasa, Davie and Mental sat round a table on a fitted seat. On the table were Mental's, Kelly's and Louise's Guinness, Davie's Special and Terasa's Moscow Mule.

Archie grabbed a couple of short, backless stools and placed them in front of the table. He sat nearest Louise.

'How long you been in?' asked Richard.

Mental indicated the empty section of his glass with thumb and forefinger and said, 'Half an hour. We were just talking about the proposed trip to Live Aid. It should be some day if it all comes off.'

'I'm not sure about some aspects of this stuff,' said Kelly. 'See at the end of parties when they put on *Feed the World*, I feel that I should scream.' Kelly wore a white T-shirt, plain jeans and the raincoat her brother wore to the boxing. A simple gold cross hung around her neck.

Archie lit a cigarette.

'We'll have to think about money if we're going,' said Terasa. She was dressed as she had been the previous evening but she didn't look as glamorous. 'We need an automatic.'

'That's what I like about you, Terasa, there's no subtlety to your bullshit, it's just good old-fashioned nonsense,' said Mental.

'You misunderstand me, I'm not being sick. If it was the choice of going to Live Aid or having a washing machine, I'd choose the washing machine. I know it's mundane and Live Aid will be history but that's the way I feel. I also have some doubt over whether the responsibility for the starving should be carried out by charity.'

'They should sell off the Royal Family and all their assets,' said Kelly. 'The most important thing about our trip is to remember that it's being organised by an arsehole.'

'Stop slagging off Stevie,' said Mental. 'The welfare of the needy and starving shouldn't be the responsibility of charity, though.'

Louise sipped at her Guinness listening intently. If she could have taken notes she would have. She worked with Kelly. She was seventeen years old. Her eyes were very soft and gave away her age. When she spoke, it was in short, nervous bursts as if anticipating marks for originality, presentation and content. Her hair was short and black with a fringe teasing her eyes. She wore a salmon-pink dress and an old Levi jacket. The hem of the dress had a stain at the top of the knee. Archie noticed the stain; he wanted to rub the stain. People were talking about the politics of starvation and he wanted to rub the stain on a dress. Archie prayed he didn't get an erection and inhaled his cigarette.

'I'm not saying that you alone have a responsibility . . .' Mental was in full flow. He wore ordinary Levi's and a black T-shirt.

'You're a fine one to talk about responsibility,' interrupted Terasa. 'You've never had any.'

'Stop slagging my wee brother, you. I remember the day he was responsible. It was a Tuesday.'

135

'When was this?' said Mental failing to get the joke. 'Oh, very funny.'

Archie was worried that Terasa was going to start slagging everybody. She looked as if she was in one of those moods. He tried to think of something to say: work, they've probably done that; TV, boring; sport, too macho; gossip, do I know any gossip? Come on, think of something. Something true, something brief, something sociable.

'Did you finish up at that restaurant?' Kelly asked Richard.

'Ah-ha. Last Saturday. Some of the smells were driving Dostoyevsky daft.' Mention of the world's greatest canine made everyone smile.

'I had a battle with him last night,' said Archie.

'So I heard,' said Terasa. 'I heard you nearly got beat and chickened out while you were ahead.'

Archie smiled and shook his head. No way.

'Well,' said Davie, 'I'm away to feed some money into the machines. You can't get any sicker than that.'

'Hold on, I'll come with you,' said The Kid.

'Who's that?' asked Archie, referring to the record being played.

'Little Anthony and the Imperials,' said Richard. Little Anthony sung 'And I think I'm going out of my head/Over you'.

'He gets mentioned on that Tom Waits LP, eh?'

'I like Tom Waits,' said Louise really quickly. 'Have you got the *One from the Heart* soundtrack? That's really good.' Archie thought she fancied Richard. She always went out of her way to speak to him.

'No. I've got the film videoed, though.' Richard was embarrassed, as much at not owning the LP as being spoken to by a pretty girl several years his junior.

Archie had seen the film at Richard's. He thought it was okay. Films were never less than 'okay'. More of an idea than an observation. Everybody said that Nastassja Kinski was very good-looking. Archie wasn't so sure. She looked pretty thick. Louise was better looking.

'Hey, look. It's Sheila Stewart, I haven't seen her for years.' Kelly waved at the couple that entered. 'Mind her at Lisbon Court, Archie?' Archie nodded. 'When we stayed at Lisbon Court,' Kelly put her hand over her mouth but she spoke at the same volume, as if keeping a secret from lip-readers rather than listeners. 'We were all really young at the time — pre-school, like — and Sheila Stewart would sit in puddles. I'm not joking. You would see her sitting at the window watching the rain come down, and when it finished whoooosh down the stairs, out the flat, find a big puddle, lift up her wee skirt, and splat! She loved it. She sat there for ages, giggling away. She would stay there for hours.'

'She really did,' said Archie. 'Her mum used to beat shit out of her but she kept on doing it.'

'I think that's her husband with the Wrangler cords,' pointed out Kelly.

Everyone at the table looked at Sheila Stewart. If people were to be rated on a scale of one to ten on the likelihood of having spent their formative years in a puddle, she would have rated one. More like the sort of person that went around shooting such deviants.

Mental and Davie returned.

'See who's in?' said Mental. Davie gave a handful of 10ps to Terasa and said, 'Put these in your bag.' 'The puddle-sitter,' continued Mental, 'or acne-arse as you christened her.'

'It's true,' said Kelly, hand over the mouth again. 'I met her at the baths once. And afterwards I seen her bum. It was absolutely covered in plooks, millions of them! I'm sure it was all the time she spent in a puddle.'

Eyes turned on Sheila Stewart again. Archie recoiled in horror. An unpleasant vision, to be sure.

'Bob says he'll play *Never Understand* for us,' said Mental.

'Great,' said Richard.

'Magic,' said Archie.

'The Jesus and Mary Chain are just silly wee boys,' said Kelly. 'It's like science fiction and horror comics. It's got that same kind of masculine appeal, wee boy appeal.'

'It's not like punk,' said Terasa. 'Punk never alienated girls.'

'That's true,' agreed Kelly. 'It's back to role-playing.

Women are either submissive or neurotic.'

'That's the trouble, sister. I'm out playing the field and that's acceptable. The only way for it to be acceptable for women is for them to do it too. It's the female attitude that has to change. See feminists and blacks, they'll never criticise their own. Most feminist ideology I go along with, right. But where we differ is where they won't admit that one hell of a lot of women are really thick. Your typical Saturday night disco-going George Benson fan.'

'The sort of woman you spend your weekends chasing,' said Archie.

'They chase me. They drag me into bed. They start crying at the most stupid things. Hell, I have a great time.'

Kelly raged and said, 'I don't know what you're talking about being so free and independent for. I had to bath you until you were fourteen.'

'GARBAGE, FUCKING GARBAGE!' cried Mental amid the laughter. He blushed furious red and avoided eye-contact. Guilty. Kelly sipped her drink triumphantly.

'Mental,' said Terasa, 'for all your Friday nights out chasing the wee lassies you don't seem very happy. I mean all these things I've heard about you since you started hanging about with Stevie.'

'Everything gets exaggerated because it's me.' Mental was pissed off. 'I'm all right. Okay.'

Never Understand came out of the speakers. That cheeky record. So un-rock 'n' roll; so completely, utterly, wonderfully un-Scottish, The Stooges doing the Beach Boys at Sun studios with Phil Spector producing and a little feedback. The spirit of the good.

'If you don't like that, you've got problems,' said Archie.

'It's okay, I suppose,' conceded Kelly. 'It's got a good beat.'

'A good beat,' said Mental with scorn. 'A good beat!' He thrust his gaze to the heavens.

'I was only joking,' said Kelly. 'I just said that to annoy you. Stop feeling so sorry for yourself, eh?'

Archie couldn't help but notice Louise's lower leg development. She must do exercises. Archie considered Louise to be the exact opposite of him. The first thing she ever did in her life was to win a beautiful baby competition. It summed her up. She was beautiful, intelligent and well liked. Everything seemed so easy for her. And now she had phenomenal lower leg development.

'Mind when we used to go out dancing to this record?' asked Kelly to her brother.

'What is it again?'

'"Rock me again and again again and again and again and again and again". Can't remember who sings it.'

'Lyn Collins,' said Richard. He resisted the temptation to rhyme off everything that he knew about the record.

'Did James Brown produce that or something?' asked Mental.

'Yeah. She was one of his backing singers,' said Richard.

Out of the corner of his eye Archie saw her enter the pub. Only as long as it takes a watch to tick twice but she confirmed her position as the most stunningly beautiful woman in the world. Ever. She moved.

'There's blue-and-yellow,' said Mental, rising out of his seat.

'Sit down,' said Kelly.

'What's wrong? I'm just looking at a pretty girl. I'm not a pervert.'

'I'm not saying you're a pervert. I just think it's a bit out of order to stand up and gawk at a girl.'

When she was in Archie's Modern Studies class, blue-and-yellow showed herself to be a vicious hater of apartheid and unions. The hatred of apartheid was understandable enough but the hatred of unions was more personal. During the 1970s sugar strike her grandmother collapsed and died. There was a lot of hoarding of sugar at the time and there was none to be bought. At the supermarket she got very worked up about the unavailability of sugar. On the way home she collapsed and died. Her grandmother was stupid to get so worked up, blue-and-yellow knew, but that was the purpose of the strike, to get people worked up. She also couldn't stand the way the bucketmen never shut the back gate because they weren't paid to. Blue-and-yellow was smarter than Archie but her academic career faltered through too much partying.

'You can never see the outline of her underwear,' said Terasa. 'Even when she wears a T-shirt. I can't understand it.'

It was like that at school, Archie said to himself. You could tell the day that every other girl changed from vest to bra but not her.

'It's just stereotyped good looks,' said Kelly. 'Skinny with high cheek bones, that tiny wee arse of hers.'

'I like her coat,' said Richard. It was a three-quarter-length red wool coat.

'I seen it at that sale at Wilson's,' said Kelly. 'You have to be ridiculously thin to wear that or else you end up looking like Liz Taylor.'

'Being skinny is one problem you don't have, sister.'

'Shut up, you. Our family has a great tradition for being big-boned.'

'My arse. I've been a member of our family as long as you have and that shit's never affected me.'

Louise grabbed a lump of Kelly's gut with her thumb and forefinger. She shook the gut up and down, nodding as she did so and said, 'Oh, you're fat, Kelly.' Louise laughed, more of a cackle really.

Kelly was fuming. 'At least I don't spend an hour every day in front of a mirror going XOXOXOXOXOXOXOXO.' She said the letters venomously to emphasise the exercise. Archie could see her fillings. 'And she works out with weights,' hand over mouth again. 'She gives more attention to her nails than Harley Street gives the Queen Mother. And she does buttock-clenching. I mean buttock-clenching?'

'What's wrong with that?' pointed out Mental. 'Better than being fat. Anything's better than being fat.'

Archie wondered what buttock-clenching was. He clenched his buttocks. Was that it? He wondered if Louise clenched her buttocks. He wondered if Louise would mind if he spent the next three years rubbing the stain on her dress.

'She's taking off her coat,' said Mental standing up again. 'Is she wearing it? Nah, shit.'

'She hasn't worn it for years,' said Kelly. 'It'll be dusters by now.'

Seventeen

'You want to help me get the drinks in, Louise?' asked Kelly downing her drink.

'Okay.' Louise stood up and smoothed her dress, touching the stain as she did so.

Terasa handed Kelly a couple of pound notes and said, 'Just get us the same again.'

'We'll just get our own,' said Richard.

'What you really mean is that you don't want to buy us a drink,' said Terasa. 'You're mean, you know that.'

'I'm not mean. I'll buy you drinks if you want them. It's easier this way.'

'Do you want a drink?' Louise asked Richard directly. She really fancies him, decided Archie.

'No, thank you,' said Richard without looking up. Kelly and Louise headed off to the bar.

'Oh, God. Here they come,' said Mental. 'Homo city.'

Archie turned his head to his left. It was the rugby club. There were seven of them. Five were wearing the club's sky-blue V-neck sweater. They grinned like idiots, pushing each other and talking overloudly.

'The biggest pervert of the lot,' said Davie indicating the man now entering the bar. 'I hate that bastard.'

'Mr John Whitelaw,' said Archie without looking. Davie nodded. John Whitelaw was the PE teacher at the High School. He introduced generations of schoolchildren to shower rituals and practical jokes. Some thought he was a good laugh, one of the lads. Others thought he made Yukio Mishima look like Quentin Crisp. Archie watched Whitelaw approach the bar. He grabbed Mercer and Ball, a buttock in each hand.

'For fuck's sake,' cried The Mental Kid.

'Homophobic,' accused Richard.

'Uh-uh. No way. If it was some guy grabbing some lassie by the tits, I would be equally offended. They're not homos anyway. Homos are usually cool. Monty Clift was a homo.' Mental tried to look humble before delivering the punchline. 'I look like Monty Clift, a wee bit.'

'You look more like Mel Gibson,' said Terasa. Whether she said that to tease Mental or Davie, neither or both, Archie didn't know.

'Wee Stevie used to be in the rugby club, eh?' said Archie.

Mental blew hard and said, 'And does he have some stories. You know what they do in the scrum . . .'

Kelly and Louise returned. They distributed the drinks. Louise removed seven packets of cheese and onion crisps from her bag. 'If you won't accept a drink then you can have a packet of crisps.' She flung two packets in the general direction of Archie and Richard.

'Thank you,' said Richard. She's trying to make him say sorry so they can become pals, Archie decided.

'She was getting chatted up at the bar,' said Kelly pointing to Louise.

'I wasn't. It was just a guy I used to know.' Louise lowered her eyelids as she answered.

'That bastard pleb Danny Morrison was at the bar,' continued Kelly. Archie recalled Danny Morrison: a stupid-looking bloke who wore muscle-sleeve T-shirts yet owned no muscles.

'It is to your eternal shame that you were dumped by something that gawkit, sister.'

'I could kill him,' said Kelly.

'I can never understand why you have so much animosity between old boyfriends and girlfriends,' said Louise. 'I always get on really well with all my old boyfriends.'

There was silence for a few seconds then Mental had a gook look around and let loose his sure-fire conversation starter, 'This place is dead.'

Terasa dipped her fingers in Richard's pint and flicked the liquid over Mental. She put her fingers in her mouth and licked and sucked them.

'That fairly livened up the proceedings,' said Richard adopting the Rev. I. M. Jolly's drawl.

'The bar's getting busy,' said Kelly munching her crisps. 'Sheila Stewart completely ignored me. Her husband looks a bit of a dickhead. He's got a wart on the side of his nose.'

The crisps were devoured without recourse to etiquette. They don't eat crisps in *Dynasty*.

Mental finished his crisps and had the bag tied in a bow before anyone else had reached halfway. If he was really bored, he would have blown up the bag and exploded it. He decided to vent his disdain on the rugby club. 'I hate rugby.' He waited for someone to challenge this assertion. Nobody did so he continued. 'All those poxy rules. I love seeing Scotland getting beat at anything but see when they get beat at rugby . . . oh, it's great. I go daft. Just the thought of it makes me feel good. Magic. I love it.'

Archie could see the reflection of the rugby players in the window. He recalled fighting Mercer in the toilet and smiled at the memory. There was no smile for Mr John Whitelaw, though. Showering after a PE class at school one day Archie had the feeling he was being watched. He turned round to see Whitelaw looking at him. Whitelaw did not avert his gaze. A few years later Archie stayed in one night to tape the new Fall session off the John Peel show. One of the songs contained a reference to Peel. It was called *New Puritan*. Peel was upset and said, 'If you think something's about you, it's about you.' And if you think someone's staring at you, they're staring at you. Archie wished he'd never taped that session. Davie had an aversion to Whitelaw over a practical joke that was played on him when he played for the school rugby team.

Archie finished his drink and turned to Richard. 'Another?' he said. Archie couldn't sit with an empty glass. It was like waiting for a train that left five minutes ago.

'You got enough money?'

'Yeah.' Archie had enough money. He lived comfortably off his giro. Cigarettes, beer, *NME*, records and dig money were the only fixed payments. And he didn't drink much and he mostly bought cheap records. It was Davie and Terasa who talked of money all the time: earning, saving, spending. Terasa said that there were times when she felt like Davie's third best friend. After Mental and Archie. Archie was astonished. She said that all they ever talked about was money. Archie said all they ever talked about was football. It frightened Archie to think about how much Davie and Terasa actually did talk about money.

The bar was busy. Bob was playing Harold Melvin and the Bluenotes' *Bad Luck*. Archie had that track on a Philly compilation at home. It sounded better in the pub, though. More dynamic, more powerful. Archie positioned himself halfway along the bar. He held his money in front of his mouth and silently sang along. Had he a stronger voice he would have said something to attract the barmaid's attention. His voice, though, was weak and he waited until he achieved eye-contact before saying anything. Even then he knew he'd have to repeat the order.

Behind him, Archie could hear Sheila Stewart's horrible voice. 'Well, you know me,' she gushed. Then her husband said, 'Everybody knows that,' in a smug voice usually favoured by politicians and experts on the Portuguese money market. Blue-and-yellow was in their company. Archie stole a glance at her. She was beautiful. Archie wasn't sure what he was supposed to make of the patterned tights, though. Were they supposed to be sexy or what? There were two things Archie had eagerly awaited at school: the change from white to flesh-coloured tights and the explanation of the colon and the semi-colon. They both happened the same day. Archie expected to go 'A-ha', instead he went, 'Uh?' Legs seemed fatter and ankles looked like weightlifters' elbows. And as for colons and semi-colons . . . And now there were patterned tights. Were they supposed to make the legs look more shapely, thinner or what?

'You being served?' The barmaid addressed Archie as if he were in a daze. Her face changed into a smile when she realised he was.

'Oh, eh . . . two pints of Carlsberg, please.' Archie figured he must have shouted because the barmaid never asked him to repeat his order. Maybe she smiled because she fancies me, Archie hoped. Should I ask for a bag of nuts? If I was normal I would just say, 'And a bag of nuts, please.' But I can't. Archie told nobody he intended to buy a bag of nuts and nobody would have expected him to. He just wanted to pass round a bag of nuts. To share. The girl returned with the drink. Archie handed the girl the two notes and she went to fetch the change. He'd missed his last opportunity to secure a bag of nuts. The barmaid handed him his change without smiling at him. She never even looked at him. In the time it takes to dot an i she was attending to other customers. Laughing and joking with them.

Ahead of Archie, one of the young footballers was flaying his arms and legs in a random manner, his head inclined backward and his jaw protruding. He was doing an impression of Morrissey. Archie recognised one of the group as Robert Jenkins' wee brother. This was his fourth time in a pub and he had yet to pluck up the courage to go to the bar. Maybe tonight, though. That checked shirt made him look older.

'Excuse me,' said Archie to the dancer.

'Sorry, pal.' The dancer sat down beside his friends and continued his impression seated. He barely glanced at Archie. Archie was angry at being called 'pal'. The familiarity was contrived. Calm down, Archie told himself, he might have called you 'mister' or 'peckerhead'. Archie smiled to himself and returned to the table. Archie saw himself at the Fluid-Carrying World Championship: five second penalty for spillage, ten for collision. Archie didn't spill a drop or bump into anyone. AND THE WINNER . . . AND NEW WORLD CHAMPION!!!

'I'm not saying you're stupid I'm just saying you're wrong.' Richard was arguing with Kelly.

'Don't know about that,' said Archie, 'I've always thought

she was pretty stupid.' Archie's attempt at humour failed like a cat trying to catch snow. He set the glasses on the table. A protest from the opposition, citing a slow motion replay, showed a spillage; add five seconds. Peckerhead gets demoted to eighth and fails a drug test.

'That's what they say at work,' said Davie. 'Worth it.'

'That guy that worked with us, Wilson, his name was,' said that once,' said Kelly.

'We got him fired,' said Louise. 'I couldn't stand him. I was sure he talked about us with his friends, know what I mean.'

'He brought in a radio so as he could listen to Steve Wright,' continued Kelly, 'and that was the last straw. We terminated him.'

'You should see this new girl that works with us,' said Louise. 'All she ever talks about is guys, guys, guys, all the time.'

Kelly groaned and said, 'She comes up to me the other day and goes, "Does a car never turn your head?". I couldn't believe it. "Does a car never turn your head?" I ask you.'

'None of you layabouts been to the job centre lately?' Terasa addressed the layabouts.

'Nah, I haven't been in there this year. Honest,' said Mental. 'I'm completely scunnered with the stigma of unemployment. All those Labour guys going "Four million, four million", that's their contribution to the debate. The unemployed think this, the unemployed think that. We're all potential baby-eaters according to the media. I bet you couldn't spot the unemployed in this pub. I'll tell you something, though, you can see the effects of employment. All those fat bastards with the Wrangler cords.'

'I still think it's a good thing to make the most of your life by working to achieve things you want,' said Terasa. 'Like good clothes, a good home. Things like that.'

Mental pointed a finger at Terasa. 'I've got better clothes than anybody here. Just because generations of arseholes have spent fifty years of their lives getting bored shitless at work doesn't mean I have to. Fuck that. This isn't the Soviet Union, you know: I exercise my freedom, God, I appreciate my freedom. Does your average Tory? Does he fuck! I mean, how often does Maggie Thatcher listen to The Stooges, eh?'

'Mental logic,' said Richard amid the laughter.

Terasa turned to Richard. 'And you with all your low-life jobs. Real romantic: twelve-hour shifts down the docks. Then hoarding all your money away and walking about in gutties twelve months of the year.'

Archie feared the worst. He repeated the hurtwords over and over to himself: selfish, scruffy, girlfriend. He tried to imagine the worst so the reality wouldn't be so bad. 'And you, how many Highers have you got? People slave for your qualifications, you know that? They go on to university, start a career, get married, start a family, have a nice home. But you . . . you can't tell me you're anything other than a lazy shit; a selfish lazy shit. You have absolutely no chance of ever getting a girlfriend, you know that. Have you ever done *anything*?' Archie was never sure whether Terasa was being malicious or not. It certainly hurt. And Archie supposed that if he thought about it, she was probably right. But he wasn't going to think about it.

'At least I'm a good-looking lazy shit,' said Mental.

Archie decided to defend himself. 'I'll admit I'm lazy. I maybe could find a job if I went out and tried. But I don't like to be judged purely on that. I think I'm a nice bloke. I don't harm anybody.'

'I've never heard so much crap in my life.' Terasa looked at Archie as if he were a piece of shit. '*What!* Do you think that you are the only nice person in the world? Do you really? I've met a lot more people than you have. There's a lot of nice blokes in the world. You're not that nice, anyway. You should go out and meet people instead of sitting in your room and listening to the Jesus and Mary Chain. You'd maybe see how selfish you were.' Terasa sat back in her chair, half-smiling.

Archie wanted to say something, that the Jesus and Mary Chain weren't the only group he listened to. He refrained, though, and kept his mouth shut. It probably wasn't appropriate.

'I'm away to syphon the python,' said Mental and he was

off. While he was away Wee Stevie, his girlfriend Sonia and the-guy-that-never-talks-to-us arrived.

'How we doing?' said Wee Stevie. 'Where's The Shambles fuck?'

'Crapping,' said Davie.

Stevie wore black: T-shirt, trousers, socks, shoes and raincoat. Sonia wore jeans, leather jacket and a white T-shirt. The-guy-that-never-talks-to-us wore a blue Parka and indigo Wranglers. He was bearded with a moustache.

'Are you staying here?' asked Louise.

'Don't know. I've only got 3p fuck. Don't know what we're doing. The Cretins are playing up in Bathgate. I was supposed to be going up to see them.'

'That lot have been playing in groups since they were thirteen,' said Terasa. 'Do they never give up?'

'They enjoy it fuck. It's what they do.' Sonia grabbed Stevie's arm. The-guy-that-never-talks-to-us looked around the pub uncomfortably. Archie didn't know him very well. Archie knew that he wrote that racist shit over Wee Stevie's flat and that he said the word 'nigger' in an argument with Richard over South Africa. Richard had justified 'necklacing'. Wee Stevie said that all violence was wrong: 'Violence is the only thing that offends me,' he said. The-guy-that-never-talks-to-us said that if Richard felt so strongly about it, why didn't he just go over there? Mental said that the-guy-that-never-talks-to-us was pissed off with the non-stop coverage on the news of South Africa and Richard's attitude. He didn't mean any harm. He wasn't a racist. He was known for his short-wave radio, his love of Heavy Metal and Ealing comedies and his impressive general knowledge. The reason Wee Stevie was 'only offended by violence', said Mental, was that he had once seen a boy getting a bottle smashed into his throat. That's what he said, anyway.

'You've got some bladder fuck,' said Wee Stevie to the returning Mental. 'How you doing, my man?' Stevie cuddled Mental and kissed him on the cheek. Mental blushed and said, 'All right. Yourself?'

'Cool as fuck, cool as fuck. You digging tomorrow?'

'I'm game.'

'I get my giro in the morning so we can party at dinner time fuck.'

Mental and Stevie exchanged clandestine smiles. Friday meant getting drunk and chasing factory girls. Mental looked happier with Stevie.

'I'm into that,' said Mental. 'What you doing just now?' •

'Just staying here, I think. I've only got 3p fuck. My darling'll maybe buy me a drink.' Stevie cuddled Sonia. 'I'm away to have a megarant with Bob. I'll see you later.'

'Right, see you,' said Mental. '"I've only got 3p". What a man.'

'Does his girlfriend know what goes on on Fridays?' said Terasa. Mental shook his head and tried to stop himself giggling. 'She must be thick,' continued Terasa. 'What about the-guy-that-never-talks-to-us, does he never tell her?'

'Nah, he's a good lad.'

Wee Stevie returned. 'Fuck I came over to see if Kelly and Louise were digging the Live Aid scene and I forgot to ask them.'

'I'd love to,' said Louise. She looked up at Stevie admiringly.

'Is there something up with your eye?' asked Stevie. He bent down and ran his finger along her eyelid.

'It's my contacts,' said Louise. 'I think I'd better take them out!'

'It's the smoke,' said Stevie. 'It happens with mine as well. You sure you'll be okay?'

'Yeah. I'm all right. Thanks.'

'I'll come with you,' said Kelly. 'I don't know how you can wear those things.' She shuddered at the thought. It was like having a pregnant spider in your eye.

I suppose this is all my fault, thought Archie. Blowing smoke into people's eyes and blinding them. Cancer of the retina.

Wee Stevie walked away with Louise and Kelly. Stevie and Louise were exchanging contact lens anecdotes.

Eighteen

'It's getting busy,' said Mental.

'Have you and Stevie got some kind of bet on to see who can get her to bed first?' asked Terasa.

Mental blushed and said, 'I'm saying nothing.'

'You're pathetic . . . so's she.'

'She isn't an idiot. Nobody'll force her. She likes a good time. We'll see what happens.'

Archie looked around the pub. Most of the faces were familiar. There was no hardness about the younger ones, they were all clean-shaven and smart. When Archie first started drinking he sported four days' growth and his scruffiest clothes. He lowered his voice when he said the word 'lager'. The role-model was Rory Gallagher. Archie wondered how he must've looked. Pretty stupid, he reasoned. Everyone else dressed up, Archie dressed down. He never got refused in a pub, though. The Mental Kid had, once. It was in an over-21 bar. The Kid called the manager a 'fucking Orange bastard' and stormed out. He was only seventeen at the time but he was pretty offended at the judgement.

'I'm fed up with pubs,' said Terasa. 'People who come here all the time are worse than folk that watch telly all the time.'

'I like sitting in a pub,' said Davie. 'Don't get me wrong, I wouldn't want to do it every night. Once a week drinking with my mates, that's great.'

'Same here,' said Archie. 'I like the blethers and I like the drink. In moderation, of course. I like a good argument in a pub. When you see people arguing on telly it seems false.'

'People always act when there's a camera present,' said Richard.

'Yes, Richard, sure,' said Terasa. 'And what "right book" did you get that out of?'

'I didn't get it from a book. I read a lot, Terasa. Mostly thrillers. Two or three books a week. If you want me to recommend a social sciences book about how to get that chip off your shoulder, I'm afraid I couldn't. I don't want to be thought of as someone who reads all the "right books".' Terasa looked angry but said nothing.

'Television can be good at times,' said Mental, 'but most of it's just . . . Bruce Forsyth.'

'Well, I like lying by the fire with Davie and Horace and I laugh when the audience laughs and I give the same answers as contestants on quiz shows, even when they're wrong.'

'And I'm sure you'd love to win an automatic on *The Price is Right*,' said Mental. 'You see, that's the done thing.'

'Stop trying to force guilt on me. There are more deserving cases for that.' Archie looked up to see Terasa smiling at him.

'Do you want to tell us what happened at work today?' Mental had his eyes closed and his fingers interlocked as he asked the question.

'No.'

'Look,' Mental opened his eyes and spread his palms. 'I know you've got your problems but I can only be so sympathetic. We're your friends, for God's sake. We're not perfect but we're all you've got. You've become very private of late. You stay in all the time. You keep yourselves to yourselves.' Mental's hands toured his forehead, cheeks and neck. He knew that his concern would be interpreted as curiosity. 'I'm worried about you. I'll admit I'm nosey, I want to know what's going on. It shames me to say it but it's true. I can't help it. Maybe I can. I don't know.'

151

'I told the work that I didn't want to work beside Syme and that new guy; the work says that's okay, fine. End of story. As for staying in, I like the company. I'm proud of my house. I am perfectly content to potter about doing odd jobs and watch the telly. You will always be welcome in my house. Going out occasionally is fine. I really enjoyed the boxing the other night. I'll remember it for the rest of my life. What more can I say?'

Mental shrugged his shoulders and said, 'What did Syme do?' No subtlety just nervous interrogation.

'Look, you,' said Terasa, 'you don't care about us, you just want gossip.'

'That's not true, that's just not true.' Mental was rubbing his temples and pushing his fingers through his scalp. For someone who believed that this caused nits and dandruff he displayed a distinct lack of personal hygiene.

'Well, that's another piece of ophthalmic engineering accomplished,' said the returning Kelly. 'Lucky I had my Swiss army knife.' Kelly sat down and said in a whisper, 'And she got chatted up again.'

'No, I didn't,' said Louise. 'He just said that he'd be in here at nine o'clock tomorrow, and that if I wanted to I could meet him then.'

'Who was it?' asked Mental. Kelly pointed to the Morrissey impersonator.

'You going to turn up?' asked Terasa.

'I haven't made up my mind yet. He's really nice and he's quite good-looking. But I'm not into the boyfriend/girl-friend bit just now. I just want my friends. All you lot.' Louise closed her eyes and stretched her fingers, a smile on her face.

'Nobody chat you up, sister?'

'Do they ever?'

'I don't know what you're looking so smug about,' said Terasa. 'When Richard told you there was a book down the library called *How To Get The Most Out Of Your Good Looks*, you were down there like a shot, eh?' They all laughed including Mental. 'And there was no such book, was there? And what little prick went up to the issue desk and tried to reserve a copy?' The 'little prick' buried his face in his hands and said, 'It's about time somebody wrote that book. I need it.'

Archie took a sip from his drink. Richard was a more irritating drinker than Steve Davis. At least Davis lifted the glass occasionally, Richard hadn't touched his glass for several minutes. Earlier he talked non-stop and now he clammed up; distant and aloof.

'This is my favourite record,' said Louise. Bob was playing Sly and the Family Stone's *Family Affair*.

'What, the best record ever made, like?' asked Mental. Louise nodded.

'Good choice, but the best record ever made is *Holidays in the Sun*, no problem.'

'*The First Time Ever I Saw Your Face*,' said Terasa, 'that's my favourite.'

'*Teenage Kicks* by The Undertones,' said Davie.

'*Atmosphere* by Joy Division,' said Kelly.

'*I Say a Little Prayer*,' said Archie.

Mental tutted and said, 'So obvious.'

'Look I've got three thousand singles . . .' started Richard.

'Just name your favourite,' said Terasa, 'preferably something that we've heard of. Actually I heard you had more than a passing fondness for *Mr Blue Sky*.'

'Will you please believe me when I say I hate that record,' pleaded Richard. 'I'll name my favourites as being *Mr Cop* by Gregory Isaacs, *Brother Rap* by James Brown and the last two minutes of Linda Jackson's version of *For Your Precious Love*.'

'What's Bob's favourite record?' asked Mental.

'I've no idea. I'd presume it to be James Brown. He uses that JB's track as his signature tune, maybe he'd choose that.'

Bob was playing Cherelle's *Fragile*. If playing records was as good as life got, Archie wondered, then was Bob Johnson, Nirvana in a navy blue V-neck sweater? He certainly looked different.

'I'm getting a tape of *Repo Man* out on Sunday,' said Richard. 'Do you fancy coming round to see it?'

'Sure,' said Archie.

'Iggy does the theme for that,' said Mental.

Richard nodded. 'Fatty Jones plays on it, though.'

'I had it out a couple of weeks ago,' said Louise. 'I thought it was a bit self-consciously trendy. Quite funny, though.'

'I'll get us a big bottle of cider,' said Archie. 'That'll keep us going.'

'I'll nick a packet of biscuits off my ma,' said Mental.

'Did you see *Beverly Hills Cop*?' Louise asked Richard.

'Yeah. It got rotten reviews but I enjoyed it.'

'We had *Lenny* out the other night,' said Louise. 'That was really good.'

'It was,' agreed Kelly. 'You know what would have happened had Christ returned this century? We'd all have electric chairs round our necks! Can you imagine blessing yourself to that?' Kelly ran her finger all over her face and body.

Archie lit a cigarette and wondered if Louise would ever talk to him. This was the sixth time they'd been in the same company. I'm not good enough for you, am I? thought Archie. Too much of a weirdo, a scruff. I wish more than anything that women noticed me. Did I tell Richard about the girl with the *NME*? I certainly imagined the conversation but I don't recall actually having it. No, Mental told him, that's right . . . I think.

Davie and Terasa were talking to each other. Archie couldn't hear the words but they didn't appear to be arguing. Likewise Kelly and Louise were talking about computers and Edinburgh. Each nodded while the other talked. As polite as politicians at election time. Archie knew as much about computers as he did about cars — nothing.

'Funny,' said Richard, 'how people talk the language of their profession. I always like to compare football managers and union leaders. They're both nervous and eager to please and they end up projecting insincerity and self-doubt because their language — cliché — limits their potential as communicators.'

There was a silence at the table and Terasa said, 'You say some weird things. Why do you say things like that?'

Richard was agitated. 'Sorry. I'm just nervous, that's all. I don't like the silence. Every other table there's always everybody talking but here there always seems to be pockets of silence.'

'I've noticed that,' said Louise. 'I'm always praying that someone'll say something.'

Terasa answered. 'It's because several of our company don't work and lead extremely boring and selfish lives. Most of these people at other tables talk about their work all the time. It's the sole conversation with some people.'

'That's just the way it goes with us,' said Davie. 'There'll be silence for a minute then the conversation'll pick up again.'

'Is anybody going anywhere on holiday this summer?' asked Louise. There was silence.

'Well, we're going to Tenerife,' Kelly indicated herself and Louise.

'Dearie dear,' said Mental. 'Legs apart city.'

'I was thinking of taking a working holiday on the continent,' said Richard. 'I did that a couple of times when I was younger. It was good. The trouble now is Dostoyevky. My folks can handle him for a few days but . . . I think my mum thinks he's going to eat her. He can look like a right evil bastard when he feels like it.'

'Do they feed him flesh?' asked Davie.

'I'm pretty sure they do. I ask them not to. I don't know if I really want a holiday. I'm quite happy here.'

'Do you never get bored staying in all the time?' Louise asked Richard.

'No. I'm very appreciative of what I've got. The one thing that does appeal to me about going abroad is appreciating what other people have got, seeing other cultures.'

'I'd quite like to emigrate,' said Louise. 'Maybe Australia. We'll see.'

Archie thought hard about responding to Louise's question but he didn't. He'd love to have had memories of exotic holidays but he'd never been abroad in his life. His mother said it was because his father couldn't take the car and his father said it was because his mother couldn't stand the heat. Archie's childhood holidays were spent in Scarborough or Blackpool. He knew Blackpool better than he knew Edinburgh or Glasgow. On holidays he went his way and his parents went theirs. Around the shops he wandered, pale and lonely. When he reached sixteen he stopped going on holiday with his parents. After that he had no inclination to go away on his own. Too much hassle and he didn't expect he would enjoy himself, anyway. Whereas other people seemed to make new friends and exchange addresses, holidays only intensified Archie's loneliness. It upset him to think of Louise on holiday, she wouldn't have any trouble making friends or fitting in. Archie tried to imagine himself in Tenerife. He stopped. It was one of those things he didn't want to think about.

'I hate, loathe and detest holidays,' asserted The Mental Kid. 'I fucking loathe them! The whole thing is just laughable. These people who scrimp and save just for a fortnight in the sun. Morons, just morons. They travel ten thousand miles to get pissed in a poxy disco listening to George fucking Benson.'

'God bless The Mental Kid,' said Archie and raised his glass. Richard, Mental and Archie clinked glasses.

'And what do you do that's so much better?' Louise asked Mental.

'I listen to The Stooges and play football.'

'Some people prefer to watch *The Price is Right*, go to Tenerife and dance to George Benson,' said Terasa.

'So you think Leslie Crowther is better than The Stooges?' asked Mental incredulously.

'What?' Terasa looked at Mental as if he were a really big piece of shit. 'You can be a contrary prick at times, you know that. All I was saying was that . . .'

'Hey people, what's shaking?' Chas and Rab addressed everyone. They were friendly and good-looking in a never-read-a-book-in-my-life sort of way. They were okay guys until they decided to drink themselves unconscious, whereupon they became insufferable.

'What you up to?' asked Mental.

'Going over to *Dingbats* to see if I can party with some fourteen-year-old. Satisfy my horn, like.'

'That place isn't very good,' said Louise, eyeing up Chas and Rab. 'The dancefloor's tiny.'

'Christ, I'm not going for the dancing,' said Chas and Rab. 'I'm the wrong colour.' Everybody laughed apart from Richard.

'Is Wee Stevie Fuck about?' asked Chas and Rab.

'Yeah, he's over there,' said Louise.

'Better see about getting some shit.'

'It's not very good,' said Terasa.

'So we've been hearing. Have to try for myself, though. Try anything once — save a cock up the arse, of course.' Everybody laughed apart from Richard. Archie noticed that Terasa was going to say something, then she changed her mind. *What?* STOP PLAYING THE DETECTIVE.

'How's your band doing?' asked Louise.

'Okay. We're rehearsing the morrow night. Fancy coming along?'

'I'm unsure of what's happening tomorrow. We'll see.'

'We'll be at the community centre at eight. Come along. Check youse later, we need to shoot. By the way, the new word for a "divet" is a "spanner". Okay?'

'Right,' said everyone apart from Richard.

Archie lit a cigarette and wondered if Louise would ever speak to him. He was a bit upset.

'Oh, God,' said Mental. 'I hear with my little ear something beginning with H.'

'What are they coming in here for?' said Davie. 'They don't come in here. They never come in here.'

'Hun bastards,' said Kelly.

'The sons of Bobby Shearer,' said Mental.

Nineteen

'Big Davidson, Wee Davidson, Loathsome-shit Hunter, Syme, that new guy and his wife and Sue Morton.' If Mental had had a few more drinks then maybe he'd have laughed at them. But now he was scared.

Archie knew what they looked like. Big Davidson had said that Archie looked like an ugly girl. Archie got well fucked-up after that insult. In third year at school, Wee Davidson was the owner of fifteen jumpers. Every day he changed his jumper. They were all different colours and different styles. Wee Davidson was one of those people who stared at you when you talked to him and then said 'What?' as if he hadn't heard. Loathsome-shit Hunter and Syme were lifelong partners in hate. Hunter used to sharpen his pencil with a penknife. (Archie's was as blunt as a carrot and The Mental Kid 'invented' sharpening at both ends.) Mental said that Hunter's skin looked like Wimbledon sick: strawberries, cream and diced carrot. He walked as if he had lost too many two-kicks-of-my-balls-for-one-of-yours competitions. Every step seemed to hurt him.

'I hope there's trouble,' Louise whispered to Kelly.

Kelly shook her head and said, 'Sometimes the only way to understand you is to assume that you're really thick.

Just keep quiet and if you ever get into trouble rely on your looks, not your brains.' Louise lowered her head and looked as if she wasn't going to speak for the next ten weeks. She looked about thirteen. Archie felt a little sorry for her.

'Do you think that lassie's ever worn jeans or trousers in her life?' asked Terasa.

'She looks so pathetic,' said Mental.

'Senga said there was an argument in *"Woolies"* the other day,' said Kelly. 'That lassie was accused of switching price tags.'

Archie noticed that the girl was still wearing that dirty brown skirt.

'It's a pity Senga wasn't here tonight,' said Terasa. 'She'd have told them to fuck off.'

'She's got a singing telegram,' said Kelly. 'She gets twenty pounds for those.'

'Did you hear what happened when that guy asked for a kiss?' said Mental. 'She fucking nutted him!'

'She did not,' said Kelly. 'She politely declined.'

'That's not what I heard.' Mental and Senga were not the best of friends. Apart from once beating shit out of him, Senga always went out of her way to taunt the 'pretty boy'.

When the Huns arrived, the goths laughed at them and left.

'I'm going over to see Bob for a blether,' said Richard. 'I'll get him to play some Hun-removing music. Joyous stuff, that's what they can't stand. They want you to be miserable and blame your misfortune on the blacks and the Jews.'

'You talk a lot of shit, Richard,' said Terasa. 'Have you ever seen blood and glass? No? Well, that's where they come from.' Richard looked meek and walked away. He was going to say that he was only trying to be funny but he couldn't be bothered with another argument.

'You still got a horn for Sue Morton?' Archie asked Mental.

'Get a grip. She's a Hun-lay.'

'Mind at that party,' said Kelly, 'when Syme came up to me and told me that he loved me?' Kelly placed her hand over her mouth again. 'It was so funny looking back. I was crapping myself at the time. He kept going on about

159

Late Call.' Kelly adopted the speech pattern of a drunk. '"I always try and watch the *Late Call*. They talk a lot of sense. I like the *Late Call*." I was petrified.'

'Those guys are every bit as dogmatic as the Catholic Church when you talk to them,' said Mental.

'It's not as if *Late Call* is such an extreme programme,' said Kelly. 'You can't imagine people watching it then voting Tory.'

'That's what happens,' said Terasa. 'Like in America you've got an entire generation raised on *M.A.S.H.* and *Hill Street Blues* and they've all turned out Reagan Supporters.'

'OH, FOR GOD'S SAKE. WHAT THE FUCK IS GOING ON?????' The Mental Kid was mental. Louise started giggling. Kelly and Terasa joined in. Davie sat still, staring ahead. Archie straightened his lips to a smile.

Hi Ho Silver Lining was coming out of the speakers.

'Got a problem, cunt?' The English accent came from behind Archie. It was soft and deep, the syllables rolling into each other omitting the letter t.

'You look all right to me,' lied Kelly.

'Fuck off, cunt.' The voice was more aggressive. Shouting without parting your lips. It ravaged the emotions like a metronome.

The giggling stopped. Davie was staring at a point three feet above Archie's head. He looked pale and confused, as if he'd just landed in the tropics.

'What do you want to work with? Fucking nigger cunts? The union'll have you, cunt.' This voice had never quoted Oscar Wilde. You could measure the tension with a thermometer or barometer, cut it with a chainsaw and you'd break the blade.

'Cunt!' The voice loudened as it was going away, getting angrier. Archie felt a knee brush his shoulder.

'What a hunk,' said Kelly. 'I want a piece of that. Eat shit, shite!'

'I think he chose that record,' said Louise. 'He looked a bit upset.'

'"Upset". Let's hope he doesn't get angry,' said Mental. 'Did you see his palms? He had the Red Hand of Ulster on each of them like that picture of Jesus where they drove the nails through. That guy is completely out of order. What fucking planet is that guy from?'

'Are we going then?' said Louise. 'I don't want to stay here anymore.'

Davie shook his head.

'See guys with tattoos,' continued The Kid, 'and I don't care if it's ANC across the forehead, the whole bloody lot of them should be strung up. How the hell can you change your mind when you've got tattoos? That's what differentiates human beings from Orangemen; the ability to change your mind.'

Archie felt strange. Nervous. He said nothing when the voice said 'nigger' and he was shocked, as much by his indifference as by the comment. He couldn't figure out what his automatic reaction was and it worried him.

'The funny thing is,' said Davie, 'him going on about the union. Do you know who the union is at our place? Wee Brendan Brogan.'

'Magic,' cried Mental. 'He's a raving commie. He wears a Gadhaffi T-shirt!'

Louise searched her handbag and brought out a macaroon bar.

'What you got that for?' asked Mental perplexed.

'Right,' said Louise, 'what I do is this: I buy something like a sweet or an article of clothing, something like that, which I associate with when I was a child; know what I mean? And I see what memories it brings back.'

'Just you stick to your looks,' said Mental dismissively. Louise bit her lower lip. She broke the macaroon bar into six pieces and gave everyone a bit. 'Right,' she said. 'See when you taste this certain memories will come back.'

Mental and Kelly recalled Uncle Roy who used to bring them macaroon bars when he visited Lisbon Court. Davie and Terasa thought of the day they went up to St Andrews. It rained all day. On the way home they stopped at a filling station and Davie bought a couple of macaroon bars. Archie thought of being sick. He once bought three large macaroon bars at the market for 50p and was sick later on that night.

'Okay,' said Mental. 'What did you think of?'

161

'Right,' said Louise laying her palms on the table. 'When I was fourteen there was this guy I used to go out with, and one day we went up the woods and he said "I've got something for you", and I said "What?" and he took a couple of macaroon bars out of his jacket pocket.'

'And?' said Mental.

'Mmmmmmmmmm,' said Louise, 'that was all.' She giggled.

Archie looked round to see Richard ranting with Bob. Archie lit a cigarette.

'Right,' said Kelly, 'enough of this in-sin-uendo. Let's have a good argument. What's your favourite film, brother?'

'*Taxi Driver*.'

'*Taxi Driver*,' said Archie.

'*The Kidnappers*,' said Davie with affection.

'*Deep Throat*,' said Terasa with a smile.

'I liked *Gandhi*,' said Louise. 'Did you see that?'

'Yeah,' said Kelly. 'It was overblown crap. I'll vote for *ET* cause it made me cry.'

'How could you tell ET was a Hun?' asked Mental. 'Cause he looked like one.' They all laughed.

Archie followed the trail of cigarette burns on the curtains. The curtains were filthy after years of nicotine attack. The whole pub didn't look clean when you studied it. Going to the pub was increasingly a mixture of pleasant routine and dull ritual.

'The wanderer has returned,' said Davie. 'You missed all the excitement.'

'I seen it,' said Richard. 'I was having a debate with Sonia and Stevie. Bob was well freaked when that guy asked for *Hi Ho Silver Lining*. The guy started looking through the records when Bob said he didn't have a copy, so Bob just played it.'

'We were wondering what you would have said when that guy said "nigger"?' said Terasa. 'You being so righteous, like.'

Richard avoided looking at Terasa and said, 'I don't know.'

'Pack it in, Terasa,' said Mental. 'More importantly, what memories do macaroon bars bring back for you?'

162

'Macaroon bars, eh? There's this wee lassie comes round the flats about once a month selling them. I usually buy a couple. Dostoyevsky likes them. What's all this about, anyway?' Mental explained the story and everyone related their macaroon memories. Archie's raised the most laughter. Louise sat triumphantly as if she'd won a major argument.

'We were also on the subject of favourite films,' said Louise. 'What's yours?'

'*Taxi Driver*. Although I'd like to have seen a follow-up to *The Blues Brothers*. I never felt that the potential of those characters was fully achieved.' Archie wondered if Richard daydreamed about making a sequel in which he starred with Prince.

Archie rose to go to the toilet. He felt as though he should announce his departure so as people would realise he was away. It often happened that when he came back nobody had noticed that he'd left.

Syme and his friends blocked Archie's route to the toilet. Archie walked around them rather than having to say 'Excuse me'. Sue Morton was looking good. Archie could see why Mental allegedly fancied her. She wasn't pretty but sexy in an attractive sort of way. Archie felt physically small as he passed people. Everyone seemed over six feet.

In the toilet Archie encountered Wee Stevie and the Morrissey impersonator.

'And how's your shiteself?' said Archie to Wee Stevie. Archie used the urinal.

'Okay fuck.'

'That shit's garbage,' said Archie to the Morrissey impersonator. 'Don't buy any.'

'I got a hit off it fuck,' said Wee Stevie.

'It's rat's droppings, baked in a moderate oven for twenty minutes,' continued Archie. Wee Stevie laughed as if Archie had said something funny.

'Chris here says that that fuck Tesco was down at the Tai-kwan-do the other night,' said Wee Stevie. 'He says the big fuck's pretty agile.'

Why do people always talk to me like this, thought Archie while rinsing his hands. I'm not interested.

'He's a vicious bastard,' said Chris. 'He nearly killed a guy. Honest.'

'Are you going to buy this shit then?' said Stevie.

'Suppose so. I'll try anything once . . . save a cock up the arse, of course,' Chris smiled as if he'd just delivered the correct password.

'Good lad, good lad,' said Stevie.

'Mental's been pissing blood since we had that smoke the other night,' said Archie. Wee Stevie laughed again. A bit forced this time.

'I'll leave you to it,' said Archie as he left the toilet.

A crowd had gathered outside the toilet. 'Excuse me,' said Archie. 'Excuse me,' he said again but it was no good. Archie did what he always did in times of stress and lit a cigarette. Pretend you're Bowie. Tense and aloof. 'Excuse me, please,' said Archie and pushed his way through. He was going to have to walk through the Huns. He squeezed between Wee Davidson and Loathsome-shit Hunter. Wee Davidson pushed Archie and Archie brushed against Tesco's wife. If he hadn't been wearing his slip-ons maybe he wouldn't have stumbled so awkwardly. His cigarette brushed against Tesco's wife's arm.

'Fuck off, you,' cried Tesco's wife.

'Fuck off, yourself,' said Archie.

'Cunt burnt me,' said Tesco's wife.

Before Archie could spell T. Rex, Tesco pushed him against the bar. Hurting Archie's back as he did so.

'Okay, cunt,' said the voice.

Twenty

Oh, God, I shouldn't be here. I should be at home listening to Al Green or reading Simenon. People never see me that happy — that wonderful. I wish they would. I wish they could make me that happy. I bet Louise fancies you, pal. Probably thinks you're really interesting. Calm down, she's just a wee lassie enjoying herself. Be rational; you're an ugly, boring bastard. You're incapable of being a good time, Archie. I'm going to kill myself.

'You're a map of the Highlands, cunt.'

Oh God, this guy is big. He could really hurt me. There's a lot of people here who'd like that. Syme looked wrecked. How much has this guy had to drink? Difficult to tell. He actually looks quite intelligent, the sort of bloke who knows his cars and football. He looks like he could abuse an elephant, though. Wee Davidson's staring at me. Hey, Wee Davidson, how come you had fifteen jumpers? It's always bugged me, that.

'See this, this is the hand that hurts.'

Oh God, what am I going to do? Very clever, Richard. I take it you selected this. And to start off tonight's show we have Elvis Costello with *I Wanna Be Loved*. Love, marriage and the bride wore a blue-and-yellow dress. Oh, blue-and

yellow, I used to write your name down on a piece of
paper, kiss it then burn it. Should anyone have found the
ashes, I would surely have died. What would Morrissey do
in a position like this? Crap himself, I suppose. Were I an
artist, I would have painted you; a sculptor, I would have
sculpted. I'm a prick, I really should kill myself. Actually, I
don't think I've got much say in the mortality stakes. Is my
fag still lit? Magic. I'll take a cool puff. AHHHHHH. That's
better. Condemned man, and all that shit.

'Smoking can damage your health, cunt.'

Oh, God, I take it you used to sharpen your pencil with
your teeth. Do people like you take photographs? Do you
eat chocolate biscuits? What do you think about? Do you
have heroes? Have you heard of Paul Morley? Are you
perpetually bored out of your skull? People like you can
put 100 per cent effort into everything you do at the drop
of a hat. Anything that requires effort, you're there. It ties
in with the 'don't think about things' shit. I might be a lazy
shit but I do occasionally think. Maybe you do, too. Maybe
you've thought too much. What do women think about? Do
they daydream? What about? Not me for a start. I'm going
to kill myself. I can't understand why there aren't millions
of suicides. Life is so tough. Look at these people round
here. They've all suffered a lot more than I have — than
I ever will. Wee Stevie claims that one day a group of
seventy-six people sat on his face and farted, one after
another. *Seventy-six*. He says it was ages before he could
look at people after that. Trouble is, Stevie, that you talk
such a lot of shit nobody is going to believe your sad story.
There's the-guy-that-never-talks-to-us: are you bitter, shy,
fascist, cool or what? I want to know. The Mental Kid:
there are times when I can predict everything you say and
there are times when I think you're a genius. I'd be bloody
interested in what you write in a diary cause I haven't got
a clue what goes on inside your head! Poor Kelly who gets
dumped by everybody . . . poor Richard who got dumped by
the only person he ever cared about. Poor Davie and Terasa,
we're your friends, I can't help but feel you'd get on better if
you had other ones. Louise, I suspect you may become the
object of derision. You don't seem very strong. Ah, blue-

and-yellow, divorced and on the dole. I suppose life would be different if I had all these hassles. That's the thing, I'm completely devoid of bureaucratic hassle. Davie wallows in it, Richard spends his time avoiding it, and Mental's heard stories that would smash your kneecaps. Are you going to kill me or what?

'I'm going to kill you, cunt.'

Oh, God, there *is* something wrong with me, there must be. When I was a wee boy and I never slept after watching *Chitty Chitty Bang Bang* at the pictures, they should have done something. It was the same with that Joan Collins film where she gets buried in the tomb at the end. And that pirate film where the good guys left the bad guy buried up to his neck on the beach for the tide to come in. What absolute bastards! Was I the only person that felt drowning after seeing that? And that episode of *Logan's Run* where the android went on about his immortality. And that programme, *28 Up*. That fucked me completely. How long till *35 Up*? Is my appreciation of death that much more intense than everybody else's? I don't know. Let's have a conference. Case study: Archie.

'I'm going to kick your arse till you fart blood.'

Oh, God, I suppose that was my life passing in front of me. Where were all the good bits? Has anyone ever told you you were shy? Apart from that elephant, like. Heh heh.

'You laughing, cunt?'

Oh God, you see the trouble is that when I went to join that junior football club and they all threw stones and rocks at me, it wasn't just the obvious fascists that made me cry; Wee Stevie was there, Terasa's big brother was there, Peter Jenkins was there, Chas and Rab were there . . . and Richard was there. It's so stupid and insignificant but I'm positive that I would not be doing this now if that hadn't happened. I've never been comfortable in those situations. I was never given the opportunity. It wouldn't have made any difference. Stop fooling yourself. Al Green's better. Maybe if I spoke to blue-and-yellow she'd speak to me. Of course she would. Probably say, 'Fuck off'. I wish I had those cliché-type reactions for awkward situations.

When you're depressed and angry, sad and lonely, just
say '. . .'. You should be very wary of what happens to
children.

'What's it to be, cunt?'

And I think I've got problems. Look at you, you were
prepared for confrontation the moment you left the womb.
Everything's effort. Difficult birth, was it? And now it's your
cords, your cardigan and your white T-shirt. What's printed
on your T-shirt? 'Ulster 1690' I'll bet. That's the thing, I'm
no longer offended by you people. I've become indifferent,
maybe even desensitised. You said 'nigger' earlier and it
passed me by. I was offended like, but I didn't have the
urge to complain. Complain, what an inadequate fucking
word! This guy could kill me. He's about twice my size.
Are you sure he's eighteen? See when you were a wee
boy did you stay in your room listening to John Peel and
counting your records every night? Did you tape sessions?
No. But how many people did? Are me and Richard the
only two people in the world with the entire collection
of *NME* tapes? Richard says when you cease to spend
most of your time in the bedroom you become a boring
bastard. Richard says his living-room is just a big bedroom, a wee boy's big bedroom. I'll have another puff of
my cigarette. Ahhhhhh. Maybe if he'd just attacked me
I'd have fought back but now I can't be bothered. I've
become one of the 'I'm not bothered' brigade. This guy
does not appear to be shitting himself. Have you ever
changed your mind about anything? I have and I'm very
proud of that. Are you the big test they're making in this
documentary about my life? Are you? I think I'll just let
you beat me up. I'll kiss you on the lips — put a little
tongue in it. I'll turn the other cheek. My defeat will be
a gesture. I'll start a commune with blue-and-yellow and
Louise. Mad Archie will be dead, Mahatma Archie will be
born. I've beaten up people because they made me angry.
You know, those things that people tell you not to think
about . . . I got angry about those things. And now I've
become indifferent. I've wasted years of my life getting
upset over these things when it would have been easier
just to be like everyone else. I am no longer offended by

shit therefore I am shit. Ahhhhhh. I have no control over
this accident.

'You've had it, cunt.'

So you're taking off your cardigan to beat me up. How
pathetically ritualistic.

Twenty-one

Archie bought the black, plastic slip-ons at the market the previous summer. At three ninety-nine Archie considered them a bargain. He loved slip-ons as a child; no hassles with laces. The Asian lad at the market said they were selling like hot cakes. Funnily enough, everything Archie bought at the market sold like hot cakes: his combat jacket, his sweatshirts and his shoes. He was wearing the slip-ons because he couldn't be bothered brushing his boots, and the slip-ons were wipe clean. It was common sense of a sort.

When Archie saw the words on Tesco's T-shirt — 'Hang Nelson Mandela' — the short-lived career of Mahatma Archie bit the dust, and the world's foremost ideologically sound fighting machine was reborn; Mad Archie. The shoe left Archie's foot and fired itself into Tesco's balls. The shot was better than Davie Cooper, Davie Provan or Michel fucking Platini, anyway. As Tesco fell forward Archie swung a left hook to Tesco's nose. 'Pkkkfffttt.' Beautiful. Tesco fell with the grace of Cyril Smith coming off the parallel bars.

Big Davidson and Wee Davidson tried to grab Archie's arms. Archie, though, was Hagler-tough and on a mission from God. He punched faces, ribs and balls; harder, faster and more often. Syme retreated a bit and made a dive at Archie pinning him against the bar. Loathsome-shit Hunter swung a vicious kick at Archie's knees and Archie fell to the floor. He looked up to see Loathsome-shit Hunter, Wee Davidson, Big Davidson and Syme preparing to implant several types of expensive footwear about his person. Archie recalled the words of Bill Withers: 'It ain't the being shot at, it's the being shot'.

What is that smell? Archie sniffed. Rotten vegetables? It seemed an inappropriate word to utter as you were about to get your balls kicked in, but Archie looked Wee Davidson in the eye and said, 'Dostoyevsky.'

'Rararararargrrrrrrgrgr rgrgagragragrgrgrgrgrgrrgrgvrgrgr.'

The old saying about sticks and stones may hold true in Urdu, Latin, French, Swahili, Greek and English but in canine ... Dostoyevsky was giving it the full rabies treatment. Foaming at the mouth, he sprang from under Bob's turntables and showed why he would never be the dog in the Pedigree Chum advert.

Syme aimed a kick at Dostoyevsky and Dostoyevsky went fucking mental. *Nobody, but nobody, does that to me. You are fucking claimed pal. Square go, here and now.* Syme farted diarrhoea.

Dostoyevsky calmed down and investigated the pub. *So this is a pub, eh? Wow, what a dump! Where's the depravity? This is where it's all supposed to happen. If you're eighteen then I'm a poodle ... and I ain't no fucking poodle. A-ha, you must be blue-and-yellow, God, you're skinny. I prefer them with a little meat myself, but then I would, wouldn't I? Do you want to see me do buttock-clenching? Heh heh!* Dostoyevsky licked blue-and-yellow's ankle and Archie's heart missed a beat.

Dostoyevsky got bored and jumped on a table. He jumped from table to table and walked along the back of the fitted chairs. He sprinted across the pub and leapt onto the bar. He strolled along the bar and stared at the rugby club. *I fucking hate rugby!* Dostoyevsky growled for fully five seconds before jumping off the bar and landing beside the foetally curled Tesco.

Archie stood up and looked for his shoe. Blue-and-yellow was holding it towards him. With this shoe I thee wed . . . She was smiling. No woman ever looked so beautiful, no woman ever would. Archie accepted the shoe and said, 'Thank you.' He wanted to add 'I love you' but he didn't. His shoe was covered in mud and he wanted to kill himself. Nevertheless he had spoken his first words to her. Blue-and-yellow looked him in the eye. Archie looked back. She was trying to think of something to say. Archie felt his cheeks reddening and he bent over and put on his shoe. When he looked up she had turned away and was lighting a cigarette. Princes Street revisited.

Can I eat him?

'No,' said Richard.

Oh, go on. If you gave him fifty thousand quid he'd still be a bastard. This is your actual evil. If you believe in violence as punishment then surely I should be able to eat him? Come on. Just let me bite off his balls. They appear to be causing him a great deal of distress.

'No,' said Richard. 'And that's final.'

The pub returned to normal. Bob was playing T-Connection's *Do What You Wanna Do*. Everybody who smoked was smoking. Archie picked his cigarette off the floor. It was still lit. He brushed the filter and stuck it in his mouth.

Dostoyevsky sauntered back to the table with Archie and Richard. *Who wants to grab my dick? If you're not fast, you're last.* Dostoyevsky got petted, patted and stroked. *Come on, down a bit. Whose hand was that? Heh heh! This is great.*

'The-guy-that-never-talks-to-us heard there was going to be trouble, he told Stevie, Stevie told me. Sonia gave us a lift back to the flat and I picked up the Seventh Cavalry. We brought him back in through the function suite and hid him under Bob's turntables. Bob was crapping himself,' Richard explained.

'I could smell you anywhere, beetroot-breath,' Archie gave Dostoyevsky a playful punch on the jowls. *Watch it. Don't push your luck.*

'I'll get some drinks in,' said The Mental Kid and asked his sister for the money.

Richard turned to Archie and said, 'You do realise you started that, don't you? What were you thinking about?'

'The meaning of life and things. All that kind of shit.' Archie sounded a bit depressed. 'Things like honesty, understanding, being good to children. That's important.'

'A lot of time has been wasted,' said Kelly, 'pondering the meaning of life. Until such time as someone can explain the universe — where it ends and all that — until such time, I'm partying. I'm sure that's what God wanted. I'm not going to lose any sleep over the meaning of life.'

'I've always hated that approach,' said Richard. 'I've had it all my life: about girls, politics, acne, Susan, dandruff, everything. What happens when we cease to be offended? The day I stop getting upset and angry is the day I give a blow-job to a double-barrelled shotgun.'

Mental returned with a trayful of drinks.

'Davie has an announcement to make,' said Terasa.

'What? Have you got a date?' asked Mental.

Terasa aimed her arms at Mental's throat and faked strangulation.

'June 14th,' said Davie.

'That's Live Aid,' said Richard. Everybody laughed apart from Terasa who looked furious.

'We'll not be going then,' said Mental. 'We're going to Live Aid. Heh heh. Have a nice time.'

'Well,' Terasa adopted a conciliatory tone. 'That was just a tentative date. We could make it July the 4th.' She looked at Mental as if she was going to kill him and added, 'If any insufferable little prick is going to an Independence Day celebration, they can go.'

Davie looked at Terasa and said, 'July the 4th!' She nodded and smiled. She said, 'And it's to be a proper Protestant church service.'

'Hell. Fuck. No,' said Mental.

'Shut up, you,' continued Terasa. 'Archie's to wear a suit and decent shoes.' Hoots of derision. 'Mental's to get a new suit, not old Tam Wilson's special.'

'I'll get a new suit. I'll get a new suit,' assured Mental. 'Old George Watson's not been looking too well of late. Shouldn't think he'll make July. Only joking. Only joking,' screamed Mental as Terasa slapped him about the skull. 'Old George is taller than me, anyway.'

'You can be an unbearable prick at times, you know that.' Terasa looked pissed off with him.

Archie lit another cigarette. He still felt depressed. Nobody'd mentioned his haircut, he thought it was pretty smart. The girls talked about the wedding, Davie and Mental talked about football and Richard talked to Dostoyevsky. Archie counted the cigarette burns on the curtains. In his mind he drew lines to join them up making patterns. He didn't feel well. He couldn't remember who played right back for The Clash. Everything was in his head. And it was going very fast. He took a deep draw on his cigarette. The memory of almost having had his head kicked in now existed as though a dream or an old television programme. Archie desperately wanted someone to touch him, to hold him. He was tired and depressed. His knee was very sore and was starting to stiffen up. Why did nobody enquire about it? Archie had just beaten up an eighteen-year-old. Maybe he was the most evil person ever to have lived. The guy was lying there with burst nose and burst balls. People walked round him as though he were a dog's turd. Just try to relax, Archie told himself. Archie could see Wee Stevie and the-guy-that-never-talks-to-us smiling at him. Stevie smiled/smirked as if to say 'I saved your life. What more do you want fuck?' Maybe the-guy-that-never-talks-to-us isn't a fascist, maybe he regrets saying 'nigger'. Archie wanted to know. It was important.

'You degrade women, you know that.' Blue-and-yellow addressed Tesco's wife as she was preparing to leave with Sheila Stewart and her husband. 'It's people like you that invoke rape fantasies, not pornography. You're the submissive one.'

'COW! SLAG! SLUT!' Tesco's wife motioned towards blue-and-yellow but was restrained by Syme and Sue Morton. She sniffled as though hiccups caused her to cry.

'I don't know if blue-and-yellow's right about that,' said Richard.

'What are your rape fantasies?' asked Terasa. 'And I don't mean sex fantasies, I mean rape fantasies.'

Richard pushed his hair back. 'I have never thought about that. Never.'

'Could you imagine being touched by that girl,' said Louise, 'or do you want to touch her?'

'She's sexless,' said Mental, 'so she can't be a sex fantasy.'

'Can we talk about football, please?' pleaded Davie.

'Who are you playing on Saturday?' asked Archie.

'Dundee. It's always a hard game against Dundee. Obviously it'll require 100 per cent effort from our lads.'

'Where would football be without the word "obviously"?' asked Richard. 'Billy McNeill says "obviously" more often than Derek Hatton says "this Tory government".'

'Never,' disagreed Kelly. 'Derek Hatton is the most intensely repetitive man in the world. He's a Tory plant. He must be.'

'He's just shy,' said Mental. 'He's okay. He's an Everton supporter.'

Archie turned round and saw Tesco's wife. She looked plain. In a black and white French film she would look sweaty and sensual. In real life colour, though, she looked like a very bad actress. Archie tried to imagine her three good friends: a sister, a pal, and the wreck on the floor.

Bob was playing James Brown's *Bewildered*. It must be great to wake up in the morning, look in the mirror and say 'I am James Brown'. The thought made Archie's eyes glaze. I am James Brown.

'Is that guy going to be all right?' asked Louise, sounding genuinely concerned.

'Who gives a fuck?' said Mental. 'Let's set him on fire.' Mental seemed excited by the prospect. 'Are we all going back in the car?' he asked Louise. 'We could go for a new world record. The Magnificent Seven plus dog.'

'It was the Secret Seven and dog,' said Richard.

'The Famous Five and dog,' corrected Kelly. 'Philistine.'

'I'm not taking the car,' said Louise. 'I've had too much to drink. Anyway the record's twelve. I've had twelve people in the car.' And after a second she added, 'Did anyone hear Graham Greene on the radio the other day?' Nobody answered so she continued. 'Right. He said that we all experience too much in life. Do you think that's true?'

There was silence. Maybe that's the problem, thought Archie. My life isn't mundane enough. There's no routine. I've been out three nights in a row. And I'll probably only go out a couple of times over the next fortnight. I should calm down a bit. Relax. I've hardly read anything over the past three days either. I'll probably read for five hours tomorrow.

'I'd like to think not,' said Richard. They all nodded.

'Well, that's midnight. We better be going,' said Terasa. 'It's been a good night. We never even mentioned the miners' strike. And you can all start thinking about presents. If you want any suggestions don't be afraid to ask!'

Tesco was still in the foetal position. He looked as soft and vulnerable as an exposed brain.

'Have you tried arousing him?' asked Terasa. 'You know, give it some mouth-to-dick resuscitation.'

'Fuck off,' said Tesco's wife. Archie noticed she had a nice mouth. Every football hooligan has a mother that will never believe him guilty.

'Well, Dostoyevsky,' said Richard, 'as a reward for your services in beating the Hun, how would you like to be left out tonight and maybe find yourself a nice lady dog and step out together?'

Fuck her brains out, you mean. I'm into that.

'You're doing well giving up the weed,' Richard said to Davie.

'I know,' replied Davie. 'Should save some money. I'm going to cut down my trips to the football as well.'

'You're what?' queried Mental.

'You heard.'

'HALLELUJAH! LET THERE BE MORE JOY IN HEAVEN OVER ONE SINNER THAT REPENTETH...' screamed Mental. Three pints and he was drunk. He smiled at Big Davidson, Wee Davidson, Syme and Loathsome-shit Hunter and said, 'Never has there been a good-looking guy playing for Rangers and never will there be one. Do you know why? Cause Huns are ugly bastards. Bitter, ugly bastards.'

'Look you, I've had enough of this,' said Davie. 'I'm sick and tired of it. The day Rangers start playing Catholics will be the happiest day of my life and that goes for most

Rangers supporters. These scum here don't even go to the games, you know that? I love Rangers and I love football. So just pack it in.' Davie was close to tears.

Mental put his hand over his mouth and whispered to Archie, 'The guy's fucking cracked, man.'

Twenty-two

Outside the roads were shiny after a slight drizzle. Otherwise, it was lovely.

'Who's this?' said Mental getting down on his hands and knees in the middle of the road and running his nose along the white line.

'Charlie Nicholas,' said Richard without looking.

'No way! No way! Charlie Boy doesn't do that. Def-inettly not.' Mental adopted Charlie's pronunciation of the word definitely as a mark of loyalty.

'Look,' said Richard. 'The media would have us believe that the only people in this country who do cocaine are black American basketball players and black American servicemen. That is patently not the case.'

'Do any of your favourite groups take cocaine?' asked Louise.

'I suppose so but I'm sure that if we had access to it we'd take it as well.'

'Does your beloved John Peel take cocaine?' asked Terasa.

'Hey,' put in Mental. 'Don't slag John.'

Terasa wasn't finished. 'Do you think any of his favourite groups adopt a more ideologically sound approach just to appease him. I mean there are a lot of fascists out there.

How many of his listeners buy all the reggae he plays? And I bet they're not the ones who send in demos.'

'Look,' Richard was angry. 'Don't slag John. Okay? When the battle between good and evil comes he'll be there on the side of good.'

'His National Service'll come in useful,' pointed out The Kid. 'Princess Anne'll be there too. She knows how to kick fascist ass. I bet she's terrific in bed.'

'Hagler'll be there,' said Archie. 'Big Frank, too.'

'YESSSSSSS,' cried The Mental Kid, 'THE FASCISTS HAVEN'T A HOPE IN HELL!'

'You coming, Terasa?' asked Richard. 'The big battle between good and evil?'

'I suppose so. But we're going to look pretty stupid. A dozen or so post-punk weirdos against a couple of million fascists.'

Dostoyevsky growled.

'Sorry,' giggled Terasa. 'I forgot; we've got dog on our side.' She giggled helplessly. Archie had never seen her like that before.

Mental walked down the middle of the road, Chuck Berry style — the duckwalk — singing Captain Beefheart's *Shiny Beast (Bat Chain Puller)* in a tonelesss, almost spoken, voice. '"Bat Chain Puller/Puller Puller/Bat Chain Puller/Puller Puller".'

'Oh, Mental. Please no,' pleaded Davie.

'I just can't get that song out of my head. You know yourself what that can be like. "Puller Puller/Bat Chain Puller".'

'I still can't get over the fact that you started that back there,' said Richard.

'Maybe. Sometimes you have to.' Archie wondered whether he sounded a bit too much like John Wayne.

'I suppose like everyone else in the world,' said Richard, 'I believe that if I got angry enough, I could take anybody. The problem is that I'm forever in disagreement with everybody.'

'How is it,' said Louise, 'that a man getting kicked in the groin is amusing but the same thing done to a woman is sadistic?' Nobody answered her.

Archie looked back to see Davie and Terasa kissing. Well, winching, actually. No school playgrounds needed. Archie felt pleased for them and a little sorry for himself.

'Do you fancy going out for a drink sometime?' Richard asked Louise. She thought for a second and said, 'As long as you understand it's just as a friend. I don't want to be special to anyone. I just want my friends.'

'You mean you wouldn't go out with me?'

'No.'

'Why not?'

'Look, you just know these things. Okay?'

Archie wished he hadn't heard the conversation. Archie knew what Louise meant about not wanting to be special to anyone. That was how he felt about his parents. He still couldn't come to terms with the fact that he was the most important person in their lives.

Archie joined Mental in the middle of the road.

'Some show back there,' said Mental kissing Archie on the lips. 'I love you.'

'You're not so bad yourself. But I sometimes think that the only reason that you put up with me is because I've beat up a few people you're opposed to.'

'*What?* For fuck's sake, Archie. Go away! "Puller Puller/Bat Chain Puller".' Mental was upset nd walked away from Archie.

'Sorry,' said Archie. 'I'm really sorry.' Archie felt like shit. Mental was really upset. What goes through his mind?

'"Puller Puller/Bat Chain Puller".'

'Oh, come on. I hate it when you do this. Just because you're sexy and gorgeous doesn't mean you get an easy life, you know?'

'Too bloody true.' Mental reverted to walking in the middle of the road. '"Bat Chain Puller/Puller Puller".'

Davie and Terasa were about fifty yards behind Archie, Louise and Richard were about twenty yards in front. Kelly was chatting up Dostoyevsky. Archie stretched his stride and caught Louise and Richard.

'What you doing tomorrow?' Archie asked Richard.

'Eh, I'm going to look through my old papers and change my playlist of singles and LPs. I'll take Dostoyevsky for a couple of walks. I'm looking forward to rekindling some interest in my old papers.'

'Archie,' said Louise, 'how come you never talk to me?'

'You never talk to me!'

'I don't want you to get the wrong idea,' said Louise and Archie died a bit. Louise added: 'I never think anyone's going to be interested in anything I've got to say. Compared to Wee Stevie and Chas and Rab, my life seems very dull, you know what I mean?' Archie decided to kill himself.

'I want to get a couple of cats,' said Richard. 'I don't know why. All I know is that I want to call them Elvis and Elmore Karamazov.'

'That's stupid,' said Louise and walked over to Mental.

'I'm not going to sleep tonight,' said Richard. 'I'm the most boring bastard in the world. I hate it when people remind me of that. I've never had an original thought in my life, as Adam Ant once said.'

'Remember that Nick Drake song *The Shed*? That's you. That was pretty smart of you getting Dostoyevsky back there.'

'No. I'll always be the prick. I'll always be the McCartney to your Lennon.'

Archie repeated the comment to himself. It sounded good. In the middle of the road Mental and Louise were laughing and joking away.

'DOSTOYEVSKY,' screamed Kelly. 'Come back.'

Dostoyevsky had spotted a rabbit and was off in pursuit.

'Come on the rabbit,' shouted Mental, 'you can beat old turnip-shit any day.'

'Come on, Dostoyevsky,' shouted Terasa.

'NO! NO! NO!' cried Richard. 'IT'S WRONG.'

Archie felt okay. While the others watched Dostoyevsky he was looking at blue-and-yellow's window. She was standing there. She looked lonely. Archie wondered if she liked Simenon and Al Green. He wondered if she thought he was selfish. Ah well, Archie told himself, I've got my fresh sheets and pillowcases to look forward to.